Theodosia

and the

Pirates

Other books by Aya Katz

novels

Our Lady of Kaifeng

Vacuum County

The Few Who Count

Theodosia and the Pirates
(The Battle Against Britain)

for children

In Case There's a Fox

When Sword Met Bow

Ping & the Snirkelly People

Theodosia and the Pirates

The War Against Spain

Aya Katz

INVERTED-A PRESS

www.inverteda.com

copyright © 2014 Aya Katz

ISBN: 978-1-61879-009-5

Library of Congress Control Number: 2014909946

Cover Illustration: Colleen Dick
"Hangman's Noose"
Visit Artist Colleen Dick at
http://comix.dorkage.net/

Printed in the United States of America
10 9 8 7 6 5 4 2 1

Table of Contents

Theodosia

and the

Pirates

The War Against Spain

Aya Katz

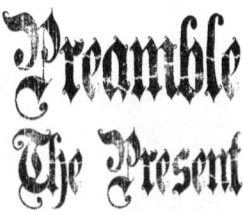

1816

Jules had free run of the deck in good weather and when the ship was docked. And they had been mostly docked in secluded spots along the bayou for several months now, as Papa had gone off inland to explore. Francisco had command of the ship, in Papa's absence, but out of deference to Maman he did not occupy the captain's cabin, as that is where Maman and Jules lived. Every once in a while Francisco would move the ship to another spot, so as not to allow their position to be known, and the small skeletal crew obeyed his orders. But once docked, he spent most of his time in New Orleans, leaving Maman and Jules and a few sailors on board.

"When is Papa coming back?" Jules had asked Maman every day since the mapping expedition, with Arsène and Papa at its head, had left. And she always replied: "He will return when he is done with his mission." But she looked worried.

When Papa left, the sun left with him. Even though it was already summer now, it was unusually cold, and an eerie fog lay over the bayou most days. Even at midday, the

1

sky was never a bright blue, but a tinge of yellow colored the view from the horizon to as far as the eye could see. Of course, one could not see very far with all that fog.

The strange weather did not bother Jules much. He had not seen many summers, so he had few expectations, but it seemed to fill Maman with dread. "I wish your father would hurry home," she said. "I don't like it when it snows in June."

"He's going to bring me a present when he comes back," Jules would repeat, every time he got the chance.

The Priest, Père Antoine, came often to call on Maman when Papa was away, and every time he came, Maman sent Jules on an errand, to go down to the galley and bring her some coffee, or to run down the length of the dock in case Tante Marie and the many cousins had come to call, or to check on the lines to see if any fish had been caught for supper.

"This weather is the sign of God's displeasure," Père Antoine said once or twice within earshot of Jules. "He has withheld his light from the world, because Man has turned away from Him."

"Really?" Maman replied. "And I heard that it was a conspiracy by the Freemasons intent on cornering the futures market in wheat and porkbellies."

"The Freemasons do not control the weather." The Priest sounded very certain in his pronouncement.

"Neither does the Church," said Maman.

"I think it's Papa's doing," Jules suggested. "It happened after he left."

Maman and Père Antoine turned to look at him.

"Jules!" Maman said. "What did I tell you to do?" There was always something he was supposed to be doing, to keep him from hearing what they were talking about.

2

But Jules always hurried back in time to catch the last bits of conversation. He could tell that Maman was afraid of Père Antoine, even though he did not know why.

The priest *did* look like death warmed over, with his long, famished face and the two white side-burns that ran on either side of it. His cleric's raiment reminded Jules of a picture of the angel of death he had once seen in a volume on theology at the bookseller's, but Maman had not agreed to buy him that book, so he never found out what it was about.

The priest had always been kind to Jules, and Jules thought that the priest's voice was quite soft and sweet as he struggled to speak English to Maman, when it would have been so much easier in French or Spanish.

"If he does not return," the Priest said, "then we will make arrangements to relocate you to a safe haven."

"Why wouldn't he return?" Maman asked. Her voice was steady, but Jules noticed that her fists were clenched.

"They are overdue," the Priest answered smoothly. "Perhaps it is nothing. But they were to have sent a messenger back with a report, and we have received no word. If the message was intercepted, then it might be reported to Washington City."

"What if it is?" Maman asked. "Of what importance is that?"

"Madame, your husband is a spy for Spain on the frontier between Spanish held territory and American lands. The Americans would not look kindly on that. And you, if you remain here, in American territorial waters, would be charged with treason if caught."

Maman laughed. "Treason? I don't think so. That's ridiculous."

"Why is it ridiculous? You are still an American, are

you not?"

"Yes. And … and a loyal one, too. And besides, we have a treaty with Spain."

The priest smiled. "Of course. But consider your position, and your father's position."

"Papa will bring me a present when he comes home," Jules said.

Startled, Maman turned to look at him. "Jules, did I not ask you to go down to the end of the quay to wait for Uncle Edward?"

"Uncle Edward?" the Priest asked.

"I came back for my silver rattle, Maman."

"All right, hurry and take it then."

When Maman was frightened, she sounded cross. Jules did not hurry. He lingered as if looking for the rattle which was in plain view on a chest in the corner. But the priest picked it up. "Could this be it?" he asked, his eyes twinkling.

"*Mais oui!*" Jules reached out for the trinket.

"Not so fast! Let me check that it is really yours." Père Antoine read the inscription on the silver rattle: "To JJL from AB. Now who is JJL?" the priest asked playfully in French.

"*C'est moi.* Jules Jean Laffite."

"And who is AB?"

"*Abuelo,*" the boy responded. "It stands for *abuelo.* It is from my grandfather. It was a present."

"Go now, Jules!" Maman commanded.

He waited patiently for the Priest to hand him the trinket. "I need my rattle first."

"Here you are, my son. It is a great gift from a grandfather to a grandson. Do you know your gandfather's name?"

Jules took the silver plaything from the Priest's hand.

"*Abuelo*," he said stubbornly, pocketing the rattle. He started to leave, but in the doorway he paused and turned. "Is Papa really a spy?" he asked.

The Priest was about to answer, but Maman spoke first. "Spy is just another word for an explorer. Like Joshua in the Bible. Isn't that right, Father de Sedella?"

He nodded.

"Your father, Jules, has gone out to explore the land and to see how it lies," Maman continued calmly. "It is no different and no less important than the work that Lewis and Clark performed a few years back."

"Indeed. God gave the land of Canaan to Moses," the Priest said, "just as Napoleon gave Louisiana to Jefferson. And when somebody on high gives you land, then you must go and explore and see how it lies and who is already living there and how best to defeat them in battle."

"Has someone given land to Papa? Someone like God or Napoleon?" Jules asked.

Maman said quietly: "No, Jules. He is only charting it, just like Lewis and Clark."

"Yes," the Priest nodded. "That is a very good comparison. Meriwether Lewis at the time reported his intelligence directly to General James Wilkinson, just as Jean will do with his report. And James Wilkinson, as always, will forward the information to the Spanish Crown."

Maman blanched. "That's not true," she said.

"What do you mean?" the Priest asked, spreading his hands. "James Wilkinson was the governor of Louisiana Territory at the time when Meriwether Lewis presented him with the report."

"The report was for Jefferson."

"One copy went to Jefferson, and another to the King of Spain."

"Jean is not reporting to Wilkinson," Maman insisted.

"Of course, he is. General Wilkinson is number thirteen. Jean is number thirteen-two-R. He reports directly to Wilkinson."

"No. No, that can't be. Wilkinson was court-martialed. He was relieved of command toward the end of the war, just before the Battle of New Orleans. Wasn't he?"

"There was a court martial, in the Village of Utica, but General Wilkinson was acquitted of all charges, much like your own father in his trial for treason."

Maman looked distracted. "I saw Meriwether Lewis in Richmond during the trial. He... he was there. He came directly there after the expedition was done. He was dressed like a frontiersman still. He didn't testify, he only stood there at the back of the room and leaned against the wall and looked very... sad. I spoke to him when court was in recess. He said he was on his way back to Washington City, that he would report to Jefferson, that he thought he might have information that would help my father regain the President's trust. But... we never saw him again."

The Priest chuckled. "He met with an untimely demise."

"They say he killed himself," Maman whispered, "but why?"

"He was going to turn Wilkinson in. He had found him out. Jefferson was going to appoint Lewis as the new governor. But... tragically, due to fits of melancholy or armed assassins – which one we may never know – this never came to pass."

"Are you saying Wilkinson had Meriwether Lewis murdered?" Maman's voice was a hoarse whisper.

"I said nothing of the sort." The Priest was conciliatory.

"But you implied..."

"I am saying that you should think of your son, Madame."

Maman had forgotten that Jules was there. But now she remembered. "Jules! Go now! Uncle Edward may already be waiting!"

"Yes, Maman."

He rushed out of the captain's cabin and ran across the deck. Uncle Edward had already tied down his pirogue, and was coming up the gangplank, a sunny smile on his face. The face of this lawyer friend of the family was as ugly as ugly could be, too thin and a little lopsided with a far too prominent chin, but Jules loved Uncle Edward almost as much as Maman did.

Uncle Edward picked Jules up as the two nearly collided in their joyful meeting. "Why you've grown so much I can scarcely lift you to the very top of the sky!" Uncle Edward joked.

"But I want to go all the way up to the dome," Jules replied, as he always did. "So I can touch the firmament of the sky!"

"Well, one of these days," Uncle Edward said. "When the sky is not so yellow and dingy. But you are getting far too big for me. How old are you now?"

"Three. Still just three. But I'm almost four!"

"Your father will have trouble recognizing you, when he comes back from his trip."

"It's not a trip, Uncle Edward. It's an expedition. Like the Lewis and Clark one!"

"Well, I stand corrected."

"Papa is like Joshua at Kadesh-Barnea!"

"At where?"

"Don't you read your Bible, Uncle Edward?"

"No, but *you* obviously read yours!"

"Maman says all civilized people should know what the Bible says, even if they don't believe a word of it!"

"Well, your Maman is a very wise woman."

"Uncle Edward," Jules said, not looking at the tall, skinny lawyer, but rather playing with the silver rattle. "Joshua reported to Moses. Meriwether Lewis reported to President Jefferson. Who does Papa report to?"

Uncle Edward laughed. "Your Papa does not report to anyone. He is a free agent."

"That's what I thought," Jules said. "But Père Antoine says he reports to General Wilkinson and that General Wilkinson reports to the King of Spain."

Uncle Edward's face clouded over and this made him look ugly again. When he smiled, one forgot that he was ugly, but when he stopped smiling, the ugliness returned. "When did he say that, Jules?"

"Just now. He's in there talking to Maman."

"Then let us go rescue her!" Uncle Edward said, and he swept toward the Captain's cabin with Jules in his wake.

As soon as Uncle Edward arrived in the cabin, Père Antoine made a hasty retreat. Citing his work load in the parish, he took his leave, but Jules thought it was because he was afraid Uncle Edward would beat him up.

"Oh, Edward!" Maman cried when they were all alone. She looked so confused and lonely and worried that for a moment Jules thought that Uncle Edward would take her in his arms to console her as Papa always did.

But Uncle Edward did no such thing. He just laughed. "It's not as bad as all that, is it, Theodosia?"

"I haven't heard from him in months. Nobody has. And now de Sedella thinks that a message might have been intercepted, and that it would implicate him, and...."

"He will be back. It's only a matter of time."

"He's going to bring me a present," Jules said.

"Please stop saying that, Jules." Maman looked tired, and she was fingering her forehead.

"But he promised!"

"I am sure it will be a very nice present," Uncle Edward said.

"Do you know what that priest said to me, Edward? He said that Jean reports to Wilkinson, and that Wilkinson reports to..."

"Why do you listen to him? He is just trying to upset you."

"But is it true? Is Jean in league with Wilkinson?"

"Theodosia, we are all in league with Jamie Wilkinson. Thomas Jefferson did business with Wilkinson. Jemmy Madison was forced to put up with Wilkinson. And I bet our new President, whoever he turns out to be, will also be in league with Wilkinson. We can't help but be. Nobody can get anything done without going through him. He's got his finger in every pie."

"But he is an evil man! He destroyed my father! And.... now de Sedella is hinting that he may have had Meriwether Lewis assassinated. Do you think that is true?"

"Well, I wouldn't put anything past him. But I wouldn't listen to de Sedella, either. He is just trying to demoralize you."

"Why?"

"To control Jean through you."

"But I have no power over Jean. He never does anything I ask."

Edward laughed. "What have you asked?"

"I don't want him involved with people like that, Edward."

"People like what?"

"Thieves and murderers."

"Theodosia, your husband is a pirate. What sorts of people do you think he's involved with?"

"He is not a pirate."

"A privateer, then. Heads of state and politicians and land agents are murderers and thieves – most of them. If you want to be a leader like Jean, or even just a lawyer like me, those are the people you deal with. The important thing is for Jean to find some land to colonize and quickly, because he can't stay here."

"Why can't he, Edward? I don't understand why he can't. He was the hero of the Battle of New Orleans. He saved this country from certain annihilation. Why can't we let him stay?"

"The political climate is not right at the moment. People in power want him gone. They're putting the squeeze on everyone who supports him. Did you know they indicted John Andrew Whiteman?"

"Who?"

"He was one of Jean's men a few years back. It was before your time. Before you were lost at sea and reborn as Emma Mortimore. Whiteman was working for Jean, in the import business, when there was a dispute with a customs agent. Some shots were exchanged."

"You mean he was a smuggler."

"Yes, working for Jean. And now they've charged him with shooting at a man and missing. It was four years ago, mind you! And he has since joined the army and served in the Battle of New Orleans!"

"But everyone who worked for Jean and served in the Battle of New Orleans received a blanket pardon from President Madison for anything they did before."

"Yes. But poor Whiteman was not serving under Jean. He was in the 44th infantry division, under Ross."

"Then why would they prosecute him now for something that happened four years ago?"

"I'm not sure. But I bet it has to do with the Patterson-Ross raid."

"Isn't it enough that they robbed Jean of all his earthly goods?"

"No, it's not enough. They don't want anyone talking about what they did. And apparently Whiteman was talking. You see, he served under Ross when the raid went down."

"Then he betrayed Jean?"

"Not exactly. They arrested him shortly before that, when Pierre was in the Cabildo. They made him testify against Pierre before the grand jury. Then he joined the army to avoid the trouble with the law. But he was serving under Ross, and he has dirt on Patterson, and so now they indicted him, and they're planning to try him for attempted murder. They mean to hang him."

"But who was murdered?"

"Nobody. That's the thing. He shot at a customs agent and missed. It's a dirty deal. They're going after anyone who stands up for Jean or Pierre. Nobody is safe. Jean has to make a clean, fresh start somewhere else. It's not just that they won't give him back his money. They plan to run out anyone who supports him. And his business in New Orleans is finished."

"A clean, fresh start? While working for *Wilkinson*?"

"You have to break some eggs if you're going to make an omelette. It will get better. Just wait patiently till he returns."

After Uncle Edward left, Maman still looked worried.

"When Papa comes back, he's going to bring me a

present," Jules said.

"I wish the sun would come out," Maman sighed.

"Papa probably made it stand still in the sky where he is, so he can beat the Amorites," Jules said. "Which is why it is so dark all the time over here."

Maman seemed cross. "There are no Amorites west of the Sabine River, Jules. And it's only a scouting expedition. They are not there to make war."

"But he could have made the sun stand still for a different reason," Jules suggested. "Maybe just so he could see better."

"Your father does not have supernatural powers, Jules."

"He's going to bring me a present when he comes back."

But when Papa returned in November, there was no present. He came in the evening and surprised Maman, and she screamed first in fear and then in delight, and Papa sat at the table and ate ravenously and then bathed and shaved his face and trimmed his whiskers, while Jules watched, fascinated. And Papa told him and Maman about his travels and the many things he had seen, so that Jules forgot to ask after his present.

"They did not know us, of course," Papa said. "For I went under the name of Captain Hillare and Arsène called himself John Williams, but everywhere we went we were well received. We proceeded up the Mississippi River to the mouth of the Arkansas and stopped at Arkansas Point. There we fraternized with the locals, most of whom are traders and trappers, and all of whom hate both the Spaniards and the English speakers with equal gusto, though they are cordial to both."

"You mean, they hate everybody, Papa?"

"No, Jules. They like the French and the Indians well enough."

"Oh. Why is that?"

"Because France has relinquished all claims, and the Indians only wish to trade. But Spain and the Americans each have plans to rule over them."

"Surely not," Maman said. "What about that treaty Jemmy Madison signed with de Onis?"

"Have you not heard what your President-elect has been saying?"

Maman was silent for a moment. Then she said: "My father has always despised James Monroe."

"The American people do not share your father's opinion," Papa said with a smile. "He came in with a landslide: one hundred and eighty-three electoral votes to thirty-four."

"That's just because the Federalist Party is done for," Maman said. "It does not reflect on Monroe."

Jules was getting bored with this topic, so he asked: "What else did you see, Papa?"

"We spent the spring in Arkansas Point, then traveled to Crystall Hill."

"Where is that, Papa?"

"The coordinates are roughly thirty-four North, ninety-two West," Papa said. And he took out a hand-drawn, folded map and showed Jules. "We traveled upriver with Louis Bringier, who is a gold prospector, and he stopped to prospect there."

"Did he find much gold, Papa?"

"Not much. But as an alchemist, I can tell you there is gold there if one knows how to look."

"Are you really an alchemist, Papa?"

"Yes, of course. I learned the art at my grandmother's knee."

Maman did not seem to like it when Papa spoke of such things, so she changed the subject. "How far west did you go?"

"We made it as far as an Osage village at the very end of the Arkansas river's navigability," Papa said, showing them on the map. And then he told them a little about the Osage Indians, and Jules would have liked to hear more, but about then Maman claimed Papa's attention again, and they made Jules go to bed early, and he pretended to sleep, but really he was waiting patiently for his present.

So he closed his eyes tight when they were wrestling. He sometimes wondered whether it was fair to Maman, when she was so much smaller. She always lost, and he felt sorry for her, especially when she cried out in defeat. But he liked Papa so much that he tried not to think why he would want to hurt her that way, and he thought that maybe she deserved it, because she was just a girl and a weakling.

"Papa, where is my present?" Jules asked at breakfast.

"Present?" Papa stretched his limbs and yawned in a self-satisfied way. "What present?"

Jules did not know what to answer. Had Papa forgotten?

"Jean," Maman, said, pouring the coffee, "de Sedella was lying, wasn't he, when he said you report to James Wilkinson?"

"What?"

"He said Wilkinson is number thirteen and you are thirteen-R-two,"

"Well, that's wrong," Jean said smiling, "I am thirteen-two-R."

"What difference does it make?"

"A great deal of difference, for purposes of the code."

"Do you serve under him? Under Wilkinson? Do you relay your reports to him?"

He looked at her soberly now. "Why do you want to know?"

"He is an evil man. I don't want you to have anything to do with him."

Papa gave her a slant-wise glance. There was an edge under his amused observation. "And he seemed like such a good-natured person to me!"

"Jean!"

"Always inquiring into everyone's health, always buying a round of beers for the crew..."

"Jean!"

"What makes you so sure he is evil, my love?"

"He was *only* the chief witness for the prosecution at my father's trial for treason. He came this close to having him hanged! He confiscated our boats, paraded him through the streets like a caged bear, fabricated evidence, bore false witness against him in open court, and when it was all done, when the charges were proved false, my father was a penniless beggar forced to flee the country, with no one to speak up for him. If you have dealings with James Wilkinson, then you betray my father, and you betray me."

"Wilkinson did all that singlehandedly, did he? He had no accomplices?"

"Only Jefferson, and you know what I think of *him*."

There was a short silence. Finally, Papa said: "Theodosia, you knew that I was taking money from Spain in order to bankroll my war against Spain. You said you understood."

"Yes," she answered softly. "I did understand. I hate de Sedella with all my heart, but I bear his presence with as

15

much courage as I can, because I understand it is necessary. I suffer brigands and thieves to eat at our table, I speak sweetly to knaves and cutthroats, but this is different, Jean. This is the man who brought my father low!"

"Brigands and thieves?" Papa said very slowly. "Am I to understand that you do not like my friends?"

"Not all of them, Jean. I like Edward."

Papa laughed. "Oh, yes, you *do* like Ed. That much we have established." He got up and banged his fist on the table. "I will leave you to consider whether this affront to your honor requires a dissolution of our partnership. For I cannot at this point vouchsafe to sever my ties with General James Wilkinson."

He got up and turned to go, and Jules scampered after him over the gangplank and all the way down to where he was untying his pirogue. "Papa, what about my present?"

"Your present, Jules?"

"You promised to bring me a present when you came back?"

"Did I? I don't remember that..."

"You don't remember?" Jules' eyes were downcast, and he was about to turn forlornly back.

"But if I promised," Papa said, "then I must bring you back a present, musn't I?"

Jules looked up at Papa, who had the oar in his hand now and was pushing off.

"Yes, Papa," he said. And the smile on his father's face was contagious.

Papa went into town and he did not return that night nor the next. Maman tried to hold up as best she could during the day, but at night Jules could hear her crying softly into her pillow.

16

On the morning of the second day, her eyes were red, and Jules felt very sorry for her.

"Maman, I am sure Papa will forgive you if you ask him nicely."

"Forgive me?" she asked, her voice full of scorn, for she was trying to pretend that nothing was wrong or that she had not been beaten fair and square at her own game. But even Jules could see that Papa had called her bluff.

"Papa is a very merciful man, Maman. Tell him that you're sorry when he comes back. He will forgive you."

"When he comes back?" she looked distracted. "What if he doesn't come back?"

"But he has to, Maman," Jules assured her. "He has to bring me my present."

"Oh, Jules," she sighed. "He's not going to bring you a present."

"Of course, he is. He promised."

When Papa came back, he was carrying something in a wiggly sack, and he went straight for Jules, ignoring Maman, who was standing on the sidelines, looking desolate and alone.

"I have something for you, Jules." He put down the bundle, and after a little bit of scrambling a puppy emerged.

Jules picked it up, and the creature licked his cheek.

"The first present I ever received from my father," Papa said, "was a terrier just like this one, and my father gave me a leather harness for it that he made himself." Papa handed Jules a little leather collar. "Here."

"Did you make that yourself, Papa?"

"No, I asked your uncle Henri to do it."

Maman was drawing closer. Like a wild colt uncertain of its steps, she was skittish, and when Papa turned from the dog to look at her, she dropped her gaze

17

and would not meet his eyes. Jules could tell that she wanted to say she was sorry, but she was too proud. She made as if to turn from him. But Papa caught her by the hand and made her face him.

"Are we still in business together?" he asked her lightly, smiling.

"Of course," she whispered.

"And you will accept James Wilkinson at our table, should I invite him to sup?"

"Jean..." she squirmed under his gaze.

"I was only teasing," he said. "I would never do that, knowing how you feel."

"Really?"

"Of course. I know exactly what sort of man he is. I don't need you to tell me."

"But I thought I must tell you, Jean..."

"For the sake of your honor and your father's honor?"

"No, Jean," Maman said meekly. "For your sake. He is a thief and a murderer and a traitor. He betrays everyone who puts his trust in him. And I am afraid for you."

"You have nothing to fear."

"He killed Meriwether Lewis."

"What?!"

"De Sedella told me this."

"Why would that priest say such a thing?"

"Because he wanted to warn me..."

"Frighten you, more likely. Jamie Wilkinson is a braggart and a coward. He never killed a man in his life. I seriously doubt he has the courage it takes."

"You underestimate him, just as my father did. He can take down a man without ever firing a shot. And he sent assassins to kill Meriwether Lewis when he found out the truth about him."

18

"I can take care of Jamie Wilkinson and of Antonio de Sedella both," Papa said. "You have my ear and I have heard your advice, and now you must let me decide how best to act."

"But they will betray you."

"Are you so sure of that? Hasn't it occurred to you that *I* might betray *them?*"

"*You* betray *them?* How?"

"They sent me on a mapping expedition. So I made maps, one set of maps for them, and another, better set for us. And I scouted the territory, and I plan to use their money to take possession of a very nice little harbor on Snake Island that I have found. It will be a port of call for all my captains to bring in their prizes."

"If it's Spanish gold that buys it, then it is *their* port."

"Not when I am done with them." And then he kissed her roughly until she wilted in his arms, and Jules looked away and busied himself trying to put the collar on the puppy. But the puppy would not stand still for it and wriggled out of his grasp and started to run away, and Jules began chasing him around the deck.

"Jules, stop!" Papa commanded.

"But I have to catch the puppy!"

"Never chase a dog."

"But why, Papa?"

"Stand still and let it come to you."

"But it is running away, Papa."

"If it is your dog, it must come to you."

"But what if it doesn't want to come back?"

"Then it is *not* your dog."

Jules stood very still, and the puppy, noticing that no one was chasing it, anymore, looked a little confused and then returned to Jules, its tail wagging.

19

"To be the master, you must first master yourself."

"Yes, Papa."

Jules thought that eventually that puppy would let him put the collar on him, just as Maman had allowed Papa to lead her into the cabin without any more protestations about General Wilkinson.

Chapter One
The Way to Snake Island

It was Pierre who now oversaw Galvez Town. Jean had gone there first in April on board the *Jupiter*, while Theodosia and Jules stayed with Marie, but at the moment Jean was wrapping up his affairs in New Orleans, while the elder brother negotiated over the prizes brought into port. A shrewder businessman than Jean, and the senior member of their partnership, Pierre was the better man for the job, and Jean grudgingly accepted the lesser, supporting role for the time being. If it were a matter of seamanship or leadership in the thick of battle, then Jean would take over. But when it came to business dealings, it was best to leave it to Pierre. The only concern was that Pierre might suddenly take ill, for every so often, since his heat stroke in the Cabildo, a spell would come over the elder brother that might totally incapacitate him. But all things being equal, in fair weather and good health and with a sunny outlook, tricky business negotiations were best left for Pierre to handle.

As with any transfer of title, there had been prior claimants, people who said they would rule that piece of land in the name of the people of Mexico or the Spanish Crown or for some other, higher cause. But Jean assured Theodosia that he had neutralized all opposition, beaten back the others, and left the new port in good hands before turning it over to Pierre. "And all in the name of the Mexican revolution."

"I don't understand," Theodosia said, as they were making their way to Marie's house for a dinner at which the Priest de Sedella would doubtless officiate, "why if you are getting money from the Spanish Crown to meddle in New Spain, you are planning to take over the port in the name of Mexican revolutionaries. Surely, Spain would not want that."

He laughed. "That is because you do not understand espionage, my dear. I have told de Sedella that the best way to safeguard Spain's interests in the New World is to pretend to be a revolutionary fighting against Spain. "

"So now you are a double agent!"

"A wily triple agent," he replied, smiling. And then he put his finger to her lips, to remind her they were about to enter enemy territory, as the door opened, and they were ushered into Marie's house.

The infant in her belly kicked, for the seed he had planted in her since his return from the mapping expedition had had ample time to grow into a meddlesome, melon sized presence. In her first pregnancy she had been proud and hopeful, but that was when she was bearing Gampy, her father's only male heir and the legitimate son of Joseph Alston. But she had been ashamed every moment that she carried Jules inside her, for despite the sham marriage to Jean, she was at the time an adultress, pretending to have drowned at sea rather than return to her lawful husband, the Governor of South Carolina. And now that Joseph Alston was dead, it was no longer adultery, but the marriage to Jean at best was only a common law arrangement and not one that would still the clacking tongues of any of the people she had known in her former life, if they ever heard of it.

She had tried on a number of occasions to convince herself that it did not matter, that what she and Jean shared was a spiritual union that transcended all earthly considerations, but the bump in her belly said otherwise. Defeated, she hung her head in shame as their dinner hostess Marie, her dark skinned sister-in-law, congratulated her on her good health and predicted, by the lie of the garment on her swollen midriff, that it would be yet another boy.

Another boy! Who needed that? Jean had two sons, now nearly grown, by his first wife. They had Jules together, and bringing him into the world had cost every internal resource she possessed, but Theodosia could tell by the way that his eyes glowed every time his only daughter Denise entered the room, that the girl whose birth killed his beloved first wife was the apple of his eye and the undisputed favorite. What could another boy possibly add to Jean's arsenal? What purpose would this child serve? It would be another greedy mouth at her breast, draining her strength and offering nothing in return. She was sure this baby would be neglected and forgotten by its father, and she saw no reason to risk her own life giving birth to it. But there was no choice.

"You will want to have this one baptized right away, my child," de Sedella said to her, following up on Marie's comment. "For in a frontier town such as Galvez, death can descend suddenly, and it is best to ensure a speedy acceptance into heaven."

The baby had not even been born, and he was already planning for it to die! Theodosia wanted to slap him, for even though she had no use for the new child, she could not bear the thought of losing it, either.

"I am not sure that will be possible, Père Antoine, " Jean said. "We may depart before the child is born."

De Sedella said suavely: "Then perhaps we should establish a church there in the new territory at once, so that your new child can be saved."

Jean did not answer, and Theodosia wondered if that was part of the deal he had made with the priest who supplied him with Spanish gold. Had he agreed to give the Catholic Church a foothold in the territory he would govern? What would his grandmother, whose husband had died at the hands of the Inquisition, have thought about that?

Denise approached her uncertainly. "May I touch your belly, Emma?"

Theodosia nodded. The girl laughed in delight as she felt the baby kick. "Papa must love you very much to have given you another child so soon."

Theodosia blushed. Was the girl that innocent, or was she goading her? It was hard to tell with Denise.

"What is the news from Snake Island?" Marie said to Jean. "Is it a very rough place? Is my Pierre safe there?"

"It is the jewel of New Spain," Jean replied. "I have had a letter from him. Things are going very well indeed. He will soon come home to you, never fear. Before I left Snake Island in his hands, I got well rid of those rascals who might have given us trouble."

"What rascals do you refer to?" Edward Livingston asked, smiling.

"Why Aury and Mina," Jean said. "The two one-time self-proclaimed governors of Galvez Town." He chuckled.

"Two governors?" Theodosia asked. "Isn't that one too many?"

"One too many!" Denise laughed. "I learned a poem

about that. Would you like to hear it, Papa?"

Jean smiled indulgently. "Only if it is on point, Denise."

"Oh, it is very much on point, Papa." And Denise got up from where she was sitting and declaimed: "There once were two cats of Kilkenny. Each thought there was one cat too many. So they fought and they fit and they scratched and they bit, till excepting their nails and the tips of their tails, instead of two cats, there weren't any."

Everyone laughed and clapped and a few cried "Bravo!" and Denise curtsied and sat down.

"Is that what you did to Aury and Mina?" Edward Livingston asked, smiling. "Did you reduce the population of governors on the Island from two to zero? Without ever firing a shot?"

"Actually, there *were* three governors," Jean said.

"Who is the third?"

"Why, myself, of course."

Father de Sedella said: "But triumvirates are seldom long-lived."

"Indeed," Jean agreed. "Mina and Aury are both idiots, so it was inevitable that I should triumph. Aury is such a fool! I told him Snake Island would make a better base before he set out. But he said 'Why not Matagorda?' Well, Pierre and I tried Matagorda back in oh-nine, and it is not a good place for a port. That was before we made our base on Grand Terre. I told him everything I knew about it, trying to make his life a little easier. He thanked me very much and said 'I think I will try Matagorda all the same.'"

"So what did you do?"

"What could I do? He is only twenty-eight, a swaggering self-important fool. I said, fine, go with my blessing. What do I care if he loses all his ships?"

"And did he?"

"Not right at first," Jean said. "Even he was forced to admit the truth of the counsel I had given him, for when he took his prizes from the Spanish Crown, seven ships in all, he found Matagorda a decidedly uninviting spot to anchor in. He sent me word that he wanted to try for Snake Island after all, so I despatched a pilot to guide him. But the impatient fellow would not wait for a seasoned pilot to get him past the sandbar. He lost five of his ships. This led to a mutiny, and he was quite a few hundreds of thousands of dollars short in prize money by the time he tried to settle down to be the governor of Galvez Town. Of course, by then it was obvious that he was not governor material, so our association sent for someone else to replace him: General Mina, a Napoleonic hero in the Spanish campaign. However, we did not tell Aury this."

"Well, didn't he notice?" Edward Livingston asked.

"For one thing, Aury is not very observant. For another, each of these two men was so conceited and self-centered that neither paid the other much attention at first, though their subordinates did clash on several occasions, leading to open skirmishes when General Mina was away on a trip to New Orleans. He came and reported to us his intention to lead an expeditionary force to conquer Mexico."

"My, that is ambitious," Edward Livingston observed. "How did he hope to manage this?"

"He relied rather heavily on the purity of his cause," Jean said, laughing. "'We shall conquer because our cause is just,' he kept saying."

"Oh," said Livingston, pursing his lips. "I believe he stole that line from Francis Scott Key."

"Who?"

"It's a song this fellow wrote to the tune of *Anacreon*

in Heaven about the Defense of Ft. McHenry. Everybody has been singing it."

"Yes, Papa, haven't you heard it? They sing it in all the taverns. 'Then conquer we must for our cause it is just' is one of the lines."

"What do you mean, they sing it at all the taverns?" Jean asked and directed an angry, questioning glance at his daughter.

Denise blanched. "So I am told." Meekly, she lowered her gaze.

"Please do continue the story you were telling, Jean," de Sedella said smoothly, saving Denise further embarrassment. "About Aury and Mina."

"Well, there is really not much to tell. Mina, fancying himself as both the governor of Galvez Town and a great General to boot, took his forces out to meet those of the Viceroy's army, was dealt a sound defeat, and was summarily executed before a firing squad in Mexico City. But before he left, Aury was so peeved with him for calling himself governor, when he, Aury, was the only real, true and proper governor, that he took all his ships back to Matagorda."

"Then who is the governor of Snake Island now?"

"As soon as Aury was gone, I took over. There were a few of his supporters left behind, and we told them they could return to New Orleans or join our cause. They happily joined. I selected all the new officers of our commune. Don Luis Iturribarria administered the oath of office to them."

"Who?" Marie asked.

"He is the new representative of the Mexican congress. We now have Louis Durieux named as acting governor, Jean Ducoing as admiralty judge, Herman

Chotaberg as shore Police Chief, Bartholeme Lafon as port surveyor and Jean de la Porta as chief bookkeeper. That should keep everything in order until I can return to properly set up the commune. Pierre is overseeing the business end until I can go back and take his place."

"And when do you plan on doing that?" Edward Livingston asked.

"I expect I will be able to finish up my affairs in New Orleans by the beginning of July."

Theodosia cringed. The baby that he had planted in her on his return in November was due in July. She had been overtaken with an urge to nest for some time now, to find a safe place to call a home, and secretly she had hoped for a house in New Orleans. There had been no reason for her to think that – Jean had given her no such hope – but the heart had reasons of its own. The thought of having to face another childbirth on board ship with no one to help her filled her with dread, and her eyes sent furtive entreaties to Jean, but he did not seem to see her. Another woman was vying for his attention at just that moment.

"Papa, you must take *me* with you this time!"

He laughed. "Not yet, Denise. It is not a fit place for a young lady."

"But Papa... Isn't Emma going?"

"Of course, Emma is my wife. But a place such as Snake Island is not safe for a young girl of a certain age. You will remain in New Orleans and continue your studies."

"But I have already learned all there is to know!"

"Surely not!" he laughed. "Have you finished reading *El Cid?*"

"Not all of it, Papa."

"Then you have not learned all there is to know."

"But how long, Papa, must I wait so far from you?"

"Until you are full grown!"

"But I'm almost sixteen, Papa! Maman married at seventeen."

"When you are married, we will talk."

On the way home, through the rushes and eddies and the outlets of the bayou, as Jean rowed his way to their temporary anchorage, Theodosia reviewed in her mind this exchange between father and daughter.

Why was Jean treating Denise like a child? Why did he give her no responsibilities? Theodosia's own father had left her as mistress of his estate at Richmond Hill to host an Indian Chief in his absence when she was only fourteen years old. He had made her an equal co-conspirator in his plans to conquer Mexico. He had promised to make her empress and set her upon the throne next to him. Why was Jean dismissing Denise and denying her the right to serve? Hadn't he urged her elder brother Antoine to come and join them? Hadn't he wanted her younger brother, Lucien, there as well? Hadn't he been disappointed when they proved less than eager to join him?

On the one hand, Theodosia wanted to tell him that a daughter was no less worthy of his trust than a son. But she was also deeply hurt. What did he mean to say when he told Denise that Snake Island was no safe place for a woman? Was Theodosia herself not a woman? Was Jean trying to protect Denise from dangers that he was happy to expose his pregnant wife to? And what about Jules? Had he no mind to the possibility of losing a small boy to the illnesses of a frontier town on the water? What if he came down with malaria, like Gampy?

"Jean," she whispered as he rowed into the darkness.

"Yes, my love?"

"Why not bring Denise along?"

"It's not safe."

She was silent for some time.

"What are you thinking?"

"Is it safe in New Orleans for her, Jean, when we are gone?"

"Why wouldn't it be?"

"There's been cholera in town, and... and also to leave her alone in that convent... Aren't you afraid of what de Sedella might do if you cross him?"

"She will be guarded by nuns. I can think of nowhere safer for a young girl than to live surrounded by nuns."

"Jean!" Something inside her rebelled at this. "Why that's barbarous!"

"Why is that, my love?"

"Don't you trust your own daughter? Don't you know that to put her virtue under lock and key is sure to backfire!"

"She is not your daughter, is she?" he asked smoothly.

"No, Jean."

"Then you will allow me to decide what is best for her."

"Yes, Jean."

She did not have the courage of her convictions, to stand up to him for Denise. For one thing, her motives were not entirely pure, and she feared that Jean might guess it. She wished that he had as much concern for her own safety and that of her children as he had for his favorite daughter. Did she have any right to urge him to bring Denise along, when it might really be motivated by a secret, stealthy desire to endanger her in the same way that he was endangering herself and Jules and their unborn child? Was it simply that misery loved company? That she hoped to demonstrate to her heart's content that she and her children were not the expendable branch of the family, lately arrived and somehow less dear? She could not tell for sure if it was her better nature or the green beast that was behind her concern for Denise, and so fear and shame silenced her, when she might have spoken up.

She changed the subject. "Jean, did you betray Mina to the Viceroy?"

"Of course not. He betrayed himself by going on a full frontal attack with an inadequate army of nary-do -wells."

"But you were so happy and cheerful to tell of how he met his end."

"Do you forget who I was telling this story to, Theodosia?"

"You were telling it to all of us."

"It was intended for de Sedella's ear."

"Your Spanish employer."

"The one who is financing my new colony."

"And you serve him well?"

"I give the appearance of serving him."

"But in fact... In fact, you serve the Mexican congress?"

"No, my love."

"Why not?"

"They can't be trusted, either. You do know that our good friend General Toledo sold out?"

"The one who wrote that ridiculous letter to my father asking him to take charge of the Mexican revolutionary forces?"

"The very one. In fact, he was willing to give your father charge of all of South America." Jean chuckled. "If only he would liberate it from the Spanish oppressor. Of course, he himself is a Spaniard. General José Álvarez de Toledo y Dubois"

"Well, what about him? You haven't mentioned him lately."

"He disappeared. Nobody knew where he was for a good long while. I made contributions to his cause. I gave him barrels and barrels full of the finest gunpowder that I mixed myself."

"Well, that was very generous of you, Jean."

"I thought so. It was meant to be used against the Spanish dragon. But..."

"But what?"

"After the fall of Cartagena, the curr made peace with the foe. He was, after all, an hidalgo."

"Was he?"

"His blood was as blue as it gets. It turns out he reconciled with King Ferdinand on the sly and was pardoned for all his sins. It taught me not to trust any man who calls himself a Mexican revolutionary, leastwise when he has noble blood coursing through his veins."

"But Jean, aren't you a Mexican revolutionary?"

"No. My heart is with Cartagena. I owe them a debt. I flew their flag on my ships while I saved the Americans. And while I was waiting to get my ships back from the rapacious Commodore Patterson and for that useless pardon from President Madison, I let Cartagena fall."

"Jean... I'm sorry."

"So I am telling de Sedella that I serve Spain, and the Mexican congress that I serve Mexico, but it is to Cartagena that I owe my true allegiance."

"But Jean... Cartagena is no more."

"It will rise again. I have sworn it."

"And what about..." She stopped short.

They were pulling up to their ship, the *Jupiter*. Jean had been so proud of it. He had had it built himself, in

Charleston. It was the best vessel he had ever commanded, and every inch of it had been paid for with Spanish gold.

After tying the pirogue fast, he climbed up to the dock and extended an arm to help her up.

"But Jean, what about..."

"What about what?" He was holding her on the deck now, his arm supporting the small of her back, and her bulging belly resting against his midriff.

"What about your allegiance to *my* country?"

"*Your* country?" he asked, laughing. "Do you own a country, Theodosia? Have you been holding out on me?"

"You know very well what I mean. I'm an American."

"Yes. And a very loyal American at that."

"I will never betray my country no matter what they say of me or of my father."

"Neither will I. I love your country."

"But Jean, how many masters can you serve at the same time?"

"Only one, my love."

"Which one?"

"Myself, of course. I am my own master."

Her head spun. Was he ultimately loyal only to himself? Was he using everyone for his own profit? Would he stop at nothing to have his own way? They had said this of her father, but it wasn't true. And she would not believe it about Jean, either.

"No," she murmured, burying her face deep into his chest. "I won't believe that. You are a good man. I know you are."

"Do you think that a free man can't be good, Theodosia?" he asked.

She was confused. "I... think that a free man can be good. I'm just not sure that a good man can be free."

He laughed. "We must work on this problem. What would Aristotle say?"

※

"I don't want to go, Edward." She was telling him the truth, a truth she could not share with Jean. Edward Livingston was her only friend here, a tie to her life at Richmond Hill, as Aaron Burr's daughter.

"You don't have to go, Theo," he said. "Just tell, Jean. He'll understand. Marie is staying behind in New Orleans. Pierre does not think any the less of her. You can stay, too."

"I don't want Jean to go, either."

"Why not? What are you afraid of?"

"I'm not afraid," she answered fiercely. "And Jean isn't afraid. But think of how it looks! If Jean has done nothing wrong, why is he leaving? I think they want us to seem to be afraid. They're chasing us away. Did you know that bastard Patterson has established a base on Grand Terre where our base used to be?"

Edward Livingston laughed. "I've never heard you use such language."

"Why doesn't Papa challenge him to a duel?" Jules' voice piped up. Theodosia and Livingston turned to look at him. They had entirely forgotten he was there. He was sitting on a barrel with the silver rattle in his hand, petting the puppy who now followed him everywhere. The older he got, the more ridiculous the rattle looked. It was a toy intended for an infant, but now he held it as if it were a weapon.

"You want your father to challenge whom to a duel, Jules?"

"That bastard Patterson."

"Jules!" Theodosia remonstrated.

"But it's what you said, Maman."

"I said no such thing. And I don't want your father fighting a duel with Daniel Patterson."

"Why not? I bet Papa could beat him!"

"Jules! Uncle Edward and I are talking. Go and play."

"Yes, Maman. But I bet Papa would bring Patterson's head to you on a plate, if you asked him nicely. You are just as pretty as Salomé." The boy scampered off, and the puppy followed before she had a chance to answer.

"I see you have moved on to the New Testament now," Livingston chuckled.

She sighed. "He does get the strangest ideas... Do you think he is too impressionable, Edward?"

"No, he is just a boy. All boys are like that. But tell me, why don't you want to go to Galvez Town? It sounds like a grand adventure. I wish I were going."

"Why should we trade Grande Terre for Snake Island, Edward?"

"Because it is further west. Everything is moving further west. Away from the corrupt centers of power. It's the relentless advance of civilization."

"Then why does it feel like a retreat?"

Livingston chuckled. "Have you broached this subject with Jean?"

Helplessly, she shook her head. "I can't tell him what to do. I dare not even try. But I don't understand what's happening. Why can't we stay? We won the war for them. Isn't that good enough?"

"It's because of the Neutrality Act, you know." Edward Livingston said.

"What is?"

"The crackdown on privateering. The need for a safe

base outside the territorial waters of the United States. I'm afraid it's the end of an era. And it's not just a penalty of United States citizenship, anymore. They've amended the Neutrality Act so that now it applies to everyone within the territorial waters of the United States."

"I hate the Neutrality Act," Theodosia said. "I have always hated it. All it ever did was penalize people for being American citizens. Any adventurer can go claim territory or be a privateer, but if you are American, you have to take your marching orders from Washington. How does that make us free? When are they going to repeal it?"

"They aren't. They're expanding it."

"But why? Wasn't it a tool of the Federalists? Wasn't it something they used to bolster their illegal and clandestine war with France?"

"Yes. And it was part of Jefferson's and your father's mission, as Democratic-Republicans, to see it repealed. And yet when it served his own purpose, Jefferson used it against your father."

"And Jemmy didn't repeal it, either. Now that idiot Monroe is using it to quash every last hope that we had."

"What's the matter, Theo? Don't you want a new adventure?"

"I want my children to be safe. I want them to be free. I want them to be American." She put her hand on her belly. "I have nothing else to give this child, Edward. Nothing to bequeath to him. I wanted at least to give him that."

⚹

"You must speak for me to Papa," Denise pleaded with her the day before the launch. "I can't be left behind here. It isn't fair! I've waited all these years to go on an adventure with Papa. Always he said, when you are older. But I *am* older now. I am practically grown! And I must go to Snake Island with him. It is my only chance!"

"Your only chance?"

"Before I am too old," Denise said breathlessly. "Before I am an old married lady and have children at my apron strings, and all the spirit has been kicked out of me."

Theodosia laughed sadly. "Well, Denise, I am an old married woman with children at my apron strings and have had my fair share of spirit-kickings, and I am still going."

"Oh, Emma, I didn't mean it like that. But... isn't it a little hard for you?" The girl looked at Theodosia's grotesquely distended belly, and Theodosia thought she saw pity in her eyes.

"Not at all. It's a lark!" But her back ached, and she was forced to lower herself painfully onto the bed in the Captain's cabin.

"Let me go in your stead!" Denise suggested. "Just this once. Just until the baby is born. Tell Papa you need to stay, and I will come on board and take your place."

"Take my place? What do you imagine that is?" Theodosia was baffled.

Denise blushed for a moment. "That's not what I meant. I meant, I could look after Jules for you."

"Really? Look after Jules? Do you think I would send a four year old child on a trip to Snake Island by himself?"

"Not by himself. With me and Papa and Francisco and everybody else who is going."

"I am going, too."

"But you don't want to go."

"Yes, I do."

"Everybody knows that you don't want to go. The

only reason you are going is because Papa is!"

"Really?! And why do you want to go, Denise? Isn't it because of Jean, too?"

"Well, yes, of course. But it's not just because Papa is going. It's because we will get a chance to explore a whole new world and go on grand adventures and conquer and win prizes and..." She ran out breath.

Theodosia laughed again. "Actually, I wish you were going, too, Denise. But Jean doesn't want you to come. And I have to abide by his decision."

"No, you don't! No wife worth her salt ever abides by her husband's decision about anything! I've seen Tante Marie twist Oncle Pierre round her finger. And Tante Yvonne can run circles round Laurent Maire."

"That may be, but I am not like those women. I can't."

"I don't believe you. You won't ask him for me because you want him all to yourself!" And Denise made for the door. But at the door she paused and turned: "I know what your position is aboard this ship. I know full well what you do for Papa."

"What are you talking about?"

"I asked Père Antoine why I could not go and you could. He said it was for one and the same reason."

"What reason?"

"That there are no brothels on Snake Island as of yet."

"What?"

"Père Antoine said Papa needed you with him because there are no brothels as of yet on Snake Island. And he did not want me to come, because a young girl would not be safe walking about alone, since there are no brothels yet on Snake Island."

"Denise!"

"Just thought you should know." And the girl

disappeared out the door. Theodosia did not even attempt to follow. She had had the spirit kicked right out of her.

⚜

The water in the Gulf was an emerald green as they went through the pass between Grand Terre and Grand Isle for the last time. Theodosia felt something. A sadness perhaps, but it was more tangible than that. Both islands used to be their own, a part of a no man's land outside the jurisdiction of the United States. But now, they had been annexed, like a prize won in battle. Yet Jean had refused to fight the American forces that had come up against him. He had warned the Americans that the British were coming, and the Americans had sent a fleet to destroy him. He had offered to help. They refused his help and sent a raiding party, with Commodore Patterson at its head, and the 44th infantry division under Ross. They had confiscated all the goods they could find, ransacked his storehouses and burned down his buildings.

But Jean still had enough flints and gunpowder stored elsewhere to help Andrew Jackson and his forces to win the Battle of New Orleans. He had fought right alongside the Americans, Patterson and Ross included. But when victory had been proclaimed, the looters were allowed to keep their booty from Barataria, and Jean was politely pardoned and dismissed.

"Jean, couldn't we stay?" A terrible sinking feeling made every ounce of blood coursing through her veins feel heavy.

"We cannot stay. There is nothing to stay for. It is better to move ahead than to keep looking back." And he turned to look to the prow, while her gaze was still in the stern.

The islands grew ever smaller, receding into nothingness. She felt a pang of something. It was more than homesickness. Much sharper than mere nostalgia. "Oh!"

He turned to look at her again. "What is it, my love?"

"Jean," Theodosia asked, feeling a second pang overcome her, "are we still within the territorial waters of the United States?"

"Yes. Why?"

"My time is come. Do you think we could possibly lay anchor for a spell, until the child is born? I want it to be an American. A natural born American." There were tears in her eyes, and it wasn't the pain.

He nodded without saying a word and went to give the order.

Chapter Two
A Flag and a Pledge

Theodosia looked over the gunwale to see her reflection in the water. She saw a woman holding an infant in swaddling clothes. The sea was calm, and all was well, and they were en route to their destination of Snake Island. It had been three whole days since the new baby had been born. The horrors of childbirth, like the pleasures of love, receded quickly in her memory, and though she gave herself to the care of this new burden without complaint, she was assailed by a melancholy premonition that whatever she did for this new child, it could not possibly matter.

Her first son had been the hope of a dynasty, but he died of malaria. Her second son was the source of deep shame, and she had trouble accepting him. But this third child signified nothing. No one was glad to see him, and no one was shocked at what his existence proved about her. What if he was just another in a long line of babies and no different from all the others?

"What will you name our little American?" Jean had come up behind her, and she was startled.

"What do you mean? You always name the babies. I

have no say."

"I only named Jules because I was afraid you would give him a foolish name."

"You mean like Gampy?"

He nodded. "It would have been ill luck to name a new baby after a dead child, and since that child was named after your father, I was afraid..."

"You were afraid I would name Jules after Aaron Burr?"

He nodded gravely.

"I would never do that, Jean. No one must ever know that our boys are his grandchildren."

"Then in that case, what would you like to name this child?"

"I never thought about it," she said. "I always assumed you would give him a name. A very French-sounding name."

He smiled. "But you have your heart set on giving him an English name, don't you, my love? Go ahead, name him what you want."

The bitterness in her welled up. "Because it doesn't matter? You're giving me a say, because it does not matter what we name him? Because he's not important?"

He looked hurt. "Why would you think that? Of course, he matters. He is my son."

"And how many sons do you have, Jean?"

"Four, as far as I know."

"As far as you know!?"

"Antoine, Lucien, Jules and now this one."

"Why Antoine, Jean? Why did you name your eldest son Antoine?"

He smiled. "Well, I didn't really. You know, I was very proud to have a son. He was my first. So I called him after myself. I called him Jean. But my grandmother did not approve. She said a son should not be named after his father. It brings bad luck. So I added Antoine. His birth certificate says Jean Antoine Laffite. But wouldn't you know it? Nobody actually ever called him Jean! Always he goes by just Antoine."

"And Lucien?"

"Christina named Lucien. And I added Jean as the middle name. Just so people would know he was my son and not Pierre's."

"So you add Jean as a sort of patronymic?"

"Yes, even Denise is called Denise Jeanette."

"And you named Jules... Jules Jean Laffite."

"Yes."

"So this child, too, should have Jean as its middle name?"

"I do not insist on that. If you want to give him two English names, you may. Provided that the last name will be Laffite."

She closed her eyes for a moment and tried to imagine that she was not Theodosia Burr and that she was not the common law wife of Jean Laffite and that they were not going to Snake Island to start a new commune. She tried to imagine that she was a young girl newly married to the love of her life, and that this was their first child. What had she thought to call a son when she was playing with dolls, when it had all seemed so very far away?

"Glenn," she finally said. "I think Glenn is a fine English name."

"Then Glenn it will be."

"Glenn Edward."

His eyes narrowed, "Edward? Why Edward?"

"Why do you think?"

"You're naming him after *Ed?*"

Theodosia laughed. He was jealous! He must be!

"No, Jean. I am naming him for Jonathan Edwards, my great grandfather."

"The evangelist?"

"The scholar. Do you mind?"

"No. Of course, not. We will register the name as Glenn Edward Laffite. Born in America."

⚜

From a distance, Snake Island looked like nothing more than an empty, wild sandbar with a few little shanties dotting its coast. On closer inspection it did not look much better.

A pilot boat came out to meet the Jupiter and guide it through the sandbars, and as the shore neared, Theodosia, whose vision was never very good, was able to make out four or five little hovels. As they grew closer she noted that all the men she saw were either black or mulatto.

"How many men are there now stationed here?" Theodosia asked Francisco Similien, the quartermaster.

"Oh, there are about fifty of them permanently on the shore," Francisco said.

Jean was busy giving orders to his crew, and it was not until late in the day when he offered to give her a tour of Galvez Town.

"Aury and Mina have left behind them an already burgeoning little town," Jean said smiling at the look of dismay on her face when she saw what a ragtag kingdom he was offering to make her Empress of. "Would you like me to show you around Galvez Town?"

"Galvez Town?" she repeated doubtfully. "Why is it

44

called that?" A discussion of etymology always set her mind at ease, even in the most awkward of moments.

"It is named after Bernardo de Gálvez, a onetime Spanish governor of Louisiana," he said. "We also call it Campêche. Though my English-speaking men prefer to call it Campeachy."

"Campeachy?" she asked. "What does that mean?"

They were now on the shore, and a red-faced, red haired man was approaching them.

"Captain James Campbell. My wife, Emma."

Introductions once made, she took up her question again. "Why Campeachy? What does that mean?"

Jean hesistated, so Campbell said: "Well, I haven't the foggiest what all these Mexican revolutionary types who named it meant by that. But I told my men under me that it was an English name: Camp Peachy. Because everything here is peachy keen." He threw back his head and roared with laughter, and Theodosia tried to smile. But it was hard, because try as she might, she found nothing peachy about it.

"Look," Jean said, taking her by the hand and leading her away from Campbell. "This is where I am building a house."

"For us?" she asked, hesitating. "I thought you were against houses."

"For us and the government I mean to establish here. We need a place for the Admiralty Court, and for the council to meet, and to fly our flag off a high mast. See, they are unloading the lumber for it now."

"So it will be a kind of white house," she ventured.

"Red. I mean to paint it bright red."

"Ah."

"And there are already several shops here, where

they sell goods." He pointed to a few shacks along the shore.

"Jean... Are there any women here?"

"Women? Well, one or two. There is Madame Victoire. She runs the tavern."

"And the brothel?" she asked, lowering her eyes.

"Theo! Why would you ask such a thing?"

"Well, how many men are there stationed here?"

"About forty. Less than fifty."

"And how many women?"

"Two."

"And no brothel?"

"No brothel as yet."

"That priest knew what he was talking about."

"What?"

"Never mind."

By January of 1818, when Glenn was six months old, Galvez Town was starting to shape up. The work crew of slaves from the very first prizes that Jean's privateers had brought in had been building houses for all the men, under the leadership and direction of Juan Castro, a captured Spanish black slave who referred to Jean, to Theodosia's dismay, as "El Commandante."

"Sí, el Commandante." After every direct order. It made her cringe.

"Well, what would you like him to call me?" Jean asked her once, when, though she had said nothing, he was able to read her too well.

"I didn't say anything, Jean."

"Would you prefer it if he called me Master?"

"No, Jean."

"That is what your husband Joseph Alston's slaves and your father's slaves called *them*, is it not?"

"I wish they hadn't owned any slaves... And I wish you did not own any slaves, either. "

"I don't *own* any slaves," he said, smiling. "I only borrowed these. They are not mine."

"You mean, you stole them."

"Yes. I stole them from their rightful owner, his Catholic Majesty, the King of Spain."

"Jean! Can't you be serious for a moment."

"I *am* being serious, my love. First you accuse me of being a slave master, and then you are angry because I did not pay full price for these men."

"I have no right to say anything, and I wasn't going to," she said, turning away from him. "I can't help it if you can read my mind."

"But why does it bother you that he calls me *el Commandante*? It only means that I am in charge here."

"Why can't you use free men?"

"What makes you think they are not free?"

"Do they have a choice?"

"To work for me or go back to the King of Spain? Yes, of course. I always give everyone I capture a choice."

"That's not much of a choice, though, is it?"

"It's the same choice *you* had."

She blushed. She had had three choices: go back to her husband, the Governor of South Carolina, or to her father, a penniless ex-vice president practicing law in New York, or to stay with Jean. In fact, he had not asked her to stay. She had begged him to *allow* her to stay. "That's different, Jean," she whispered. "I love you."

"And what makes you think that they don't?"

Theodosia looked toward Juan Castro. He was talking

to one of the men under him. Then he looked back at Jean. And he was smiling.

⚜

By the time *La Maison Rouge* was completed and painted bright red, there were about one thousand men in Galvez Town, and a few more women, some the wives of privateers, including Jean's sister Yvonne who was married to Laurent Maire. It was she who eventually sewed the flag before which each new privateer was sworn upon being awarded a letter of marque signed by none other than Jean Laffite, *el commandante.*

"Why can't you just be the governor, the way you were at Barataria?" Theodosia asked.

"Because... because I've had a promotion," he said smiling. "Someone else is the governor now, and I am... just one step above the governor."

There were times when his humor was contagious, and Theodosia could not help but ask: "Above the governor? Who promoted you, Jean? Was it James Wilkinson? Or Father de Sedella? Or the Spanish Consul, Fatio?"

"Someone even higher than that," he said, his eyes twinkling mischievously.

"Who? Who promoted you?"

"I did. I decided that to be a governor was simply too low an aspiration."

"Well," she answered, "please give me a warning, Jean, if you undergo an apotheosis. I might not know and still treat you like a mortal. I wouldn't want to be struck by lightning."

He whispered in her ear: "In the event that I become a god, you will be the first to know." His warm breath aroused and reassured her.

But he did not follow up on the seduction, instead fishing out of his desk a rolled up piece of parchment and saying. "Here, read this. It will give you some idea of the government I originally set up here in April, and then we can talk of how it will be superceded soon by an even better one."

REGISTRY OF DELIBERATIONS
made at Gálvez Town
April 15, 1817

There appeared the undersigned persons to take the necessary oath of allegiance to the Republic of Mexico, under the hands of those who represent said Nation, thereby executing this act by all due solemnity.

Appearing first, the Citizen Commander Louis Durieux, who took the oath before the Citizen Louis Ituribarria and afterwards, the rest of the authorities took the oath before the said Commander in the regular manner, and to make it authentic, it has been signed by all persons present, and the said document made a record of the said Protocol with all the signatures herein together with the signature of the said Representative and at all times it will be valid and legal. As under the actual circumstances the state seal could not be had, the small seal was subsituted until the rightful seal can be procured.

Signed, Louis Ituribarria, Louis Durieux, Antoine Pironneau, Jr, Jean DuCoing, Rousselin, Raymond Espangol

Barthelemy Lafon, Secretary ad interim.

In the Bay of Galvez, the 20th of April, in the year 1817, the Military Chiefs and the Captains of the ships of war of the Independence of Mexico, met in the schooner The Jupiter, to name, with the formalities required by the authorities, which in the name of the Mexican government, legitimately protects this Nation, particularly in time of war, which they now are in with the Spanish Royalists, in consequence of which they proceed to give their votes to the following articles:

Being present by reason of a citation given to the undersigned captains of vessels of war found this day in the Bay of Galvez, we have taken into consideration the deliberations of the 17th of this month, in which was named for Military Commander the Citizen Louis Durieux, Colonel; for Adjutant Commander, the Citizen Antoine Pironneau, Jr.; as Admiralty Judge, the Citizen Jean Ducoing; for Administrator of Revenues, the Citizen Rousselin; and the Citizen Raymond Espagnol for Public Secretary, all of whom are recognized by the Assembly ad interim.

At the same time, it is decided that the Citizen Jean Fannet be Commander of the Navy of the said Port, with all the rights as is necessary in such case after various considerations, all members of this assembly having arrived at a unanimous decision about the right to collect from the prizes which are actually there or may arrive in the Port of Galvez, after a proper hearing and condemnation.

1st. The Treasurer shall pay from the Listo Bueno the Commander of the Place all that he shall need in this Port of Galvez for the support of officers, employees and munitions of war and any other expenses which are the rights and obligations of diverse officers.

2nd. That after they know the expenses, they shall retain in advance, from the actual funds the amount necessary for the payment of the month following.

3rd. That the surplus money be made to pay the debts of the government made before the date of April 15, 1817, with the expressed condition that those who are not actual employees of the said Post cannot enjoy the advantages of this decision and pay only the old debts of those who at present serve in the said Port of Galvez Town.

4Th. That the salaries of the employees and officers shall be regulated by Special Assemby and shall be written in the books of deliberations.

All has been signed before the Secretary ad interim Lafon.

Louis Durieux, Antoin Pironneau, Jr., Jean Ducoing, Rousselin, Jean Fannet, Raymond Espagnol, Parisis, Jean Guerre, Dutrieu, Denis Thomas, Faiquare, Joseph Place, Renaud, B. Lavau, Savary, Marcelin, Gilot.

Theodosia looked up from the paper, a little tired of all the legalities. "Well, I see that your signature does not appear on this document."

"No, but I arranged it all. And that puts me one step above the governor – or rather the military commander."

Theodosia laughed. "I suppose that's why the signature of God does not appear on the Declaration of Independence, despite the fact that some believe it to be divinely inspired."

"I love the Declaration of Independence," he said softly.

"I know you do, Jean." There was a moment of silence. She had loved it, too, until Jefferson betrayed her father. Now every time it was mentioned or quoted as the workmanship of the Sage of Monticello, it seemed a two-faced hackneyed, sanctimonious piece of twaddle. "Endowed by their Creator with certain inalienable rights." What happened to those rights when Jefferson had her father arrested, held without bail or counsel and paraded in a cage in front of all the rabble? It made her sick at heart remembering, so much so that she almost lost her train of thought. Then she rallied. "But tell me, Jean, why is it that these Mexican revolutionaries who signed here all have such French sounding names?"

"Oh, this is only an English translation of the French version of the document," he said, shrugging. "We had to make an English translation to file in the Federal Distict Court in New Orleans."

"Why is that?"

"Because they are accusing us of being pirates, again," he said shrugging. "But I ask you, would pirates draw up such a legal document?"

She laughed. "I suppose they might. What specific act of piracy are they accusing you of now?"

"Something to do with pivots."

"What?!"

"They brought a case against our pivots that we bought to use for gun stands."

"Really? And what are they accusing those defenseless pivots of having done?"

"We ordered some pivots for our guns, and they think we should pay customs tax on them, so they brought this ridiculous law suit. It is called The United States v. 37 Pivots."

"Did you ship them through New Orleans?"

"The customs gunboats intercepted them there."

"But failure to pay customs tax is hardly piracy..."

"They are trying their best to obscure the difference. It's they who are the pirates. They forced us to post bonds before we could take possession of those pivots. And they are calling any privateer manned by a multinational crew a pirate ship."

"Since when?"

"Since last year. So now I have to establish a naturalization process here at Campêche to make sure that every crewmember on each of our ships can prove he is a citizen of the same country as every other crewmember. To this end, I need an oath of loyalty and a flag. Could you sew me this flag, Theo?" He handed her a sketch on a sheet of paper of a flag he'd drawn.

"What do I look like, Betsy Ross?" she asked crossly.

"I don't know. What does Betsy Ross look like?" he asked.

"Old. Very old. I can't sew, Jean."

"Then your education has been sorely neglected. Denise is a very fine seamstress. The nuns are also teaching her to spin and to weave."

"Then perhaps you should have brought Denise

along."

He turned away. "I haven't received a letter from her in a while," he said. "I hope she is applying herself to her studies."

"What flag is this, Jean?" she asked, still staring at the drawing.

"Don't you recognize it?"

"It looks like the flag of Cartagena that you used to fly off the mast of *La Diligente.*"

"It is."

"But Jean, Cartagena fell. The Republic of Cartagena is no more. It no longer exists."

"It does now. Every man under me will swear allegiance to this flag."

"You want them to swear allegiance to a country that does not exist?"

He turned back to her and placed a hand on her shoulder, not as he would to a woman, but to a comrade in arms. "Countries, like gods, exist only in the minds of men. As long as men believe, then they are real. When men stop believing, then they cease to exist. As long as people believe in her, Cartagena will never die."

She remembered de Sedella's words: "Delenda est Cartago." And she remembered how distraught Jean had been when he learned that Pablo Morillo had sacked and burned Cartagena. He had been able to do nothing to help lift the siege, because Daniel Patterson had taken all the ships, and the American courts allowed it.

"Jean..." she started to say. "I'm sorry."

"It's all right. I will ask Yvonne to sew the flag."

⁂

The oath, which was administered in French, English and Spanish, went like this: "I, James Campbell, renounce my previous allegiance to any state or nation, and pledge my undying loyalty to the Commune at Campêche, to the city of Galvez, and to this flag and the republic of Carthagena for which it stands."

"Yo, Juan Castro, renuncio a mi lealtad anterior a cualquier estado o nación, y prometo mi lealtad inquebrantable a la Comuna en Campeche, a la ciudad de Gálvez, y a esta bandera y la república de Cartagena a la que representa."

"Je, Jean Durieux, renonce à mon allégeance précédente à tout état ou nation, en gage de mon indéfectible fidélité à la commune à Campêche, à la ville de Galvez, et à ce drapeau et la République de Cartagène qu'il représente."

One by one she watched the men go up and stand before that giant flag that Yvonne had sewn and make this pledge, but each pledged it in his own language and in his own manner, and Theodosia suddenly realized that they were not giving up their nationalities at all. This oath allowed each of them to remain who or what he already was, and the only thing they promised was to serve Jean with all their heart, without changing one iota of their being.

It took several days before all were sworn in, for there were too many to swear them in all at once. And James Campbell, seeing her standing there with her baby in her arms and her little boy at her side, said to her once. "Soon it will be your turn."

The idea frightened her. For inasmuch as she had stood there in that great hall in The Red House, and had felt a sense of wonder and awe at the sight of all those men pledging their loyalty to Jean, even though Jean's name was never mentioned, and to a republic that had long since ceased to exist, but would now live in their hearts forever, she could not bring herself to renounce her loyalty to the United States, nor did she want her children to do so.

What if he asked that of her? Would she have the strength of character to refuse him? And if she did, what would be the natural consequence of such a refusal? Expulsion from the Commune? Being sent back to New Orleans as a discarded wife?

She had not wanted to come here. But she could not bear the thought of leaving. When they married, Jean had not required her to swear to obey him. They both took the same oath. "I promise to go all the way to hell with you if necessary."

Would she be violating that oath if she refused to give up her American citizenship for him? How could she expect to be the only person on Snake Island not to swear an oath of loyalty to Jean? How could she possibly be exempted from this?

She saw strong men and free bow their heads and make the pledge. Nobody had forced them, and they were happy to do so. But even though she trembled in fear of the consequences, she was determined not to follow their example.

They had called her father a traitor. Even when he was acquitted of all charges, the reputation stuck to him. Her husband, Joseph Alston, had tried to distance himself from the stigma. But she would never renounce her father nor her country. And even here under the alias of Emma Mortimore, she would remain true to her country.

That evening, she refused Jean's usual embraces at the end of the day, set him down in a chair at the table, and asked, a tremor in her voice: "Would you like some coffee, Jean?"

"Coffee? At this time of night?"

"Yes, Jean. I think you should have some coffee."

He smiled. "Very well." And observing how her hands trembled when she poured him a cup, he asked: "Are you planning to challenge me to a duel?" For it was a well known practice of his to gauge his opponents' weaknesses by inviting them to drink coffee with him before every duel.

"No, Jean," she said hesitantly, taking a seat across the table from him, "I wish to discuss with you a matter of international significance."

"That serious, is it?"

"Yes, Jean."

"Well then, what is this matter of international significance?"

"You know that I am American," she said, looking down at the tablecloth.

"Yes, I surmised as much," he said, "when we first met."

They had met on board the Patriot. He had saved her from the marauding British who had captured the ship. He had saved her country, and her country had turned its back on him, once it was safe to do so. They had pillaged his property, and when he donated what was not taken by force freely to the American cause, no acknowledgement was ever made but an empty pardon.

"Jean, you know that I am very sorry about what my country has done to you."

"Yes, you told me that, once or twice. I do not hold you responsible for the actions of your government."

"That is most kind of you," she mumbled.

"What is it, Theo? What is troubling you?"

"I can't take the oath, Jean."

"What oath?"

"The oath of allegiance. I can't renounce my loyalty to my own country. I... I wish I could. But they said of me that I was a traitor... they said it of my father. And he is not a traitor. And I am not a traitor. And I won't renounce my citizenship, no matter what they do, to him or to me or... even to you. I'm so sorry!"

There was a moment of silence during which she stared at the table cloth, not knowing what to expect.

"Is that all?" he asked.

"That's all."

"Well, in that case, I will be unable to grant you a letter of marque."

"What?"

"You will not be able to serve on any of my ships as either an officer or a crew member. And I cannot grant you a letter of marque."

"Is that all?" she asked meekly.

"That's all."

"Then you won't divorce me or banish me or throw me into the sea? Or take my children away from me?"

He laughed. "Why would I do that?"

"For disloyalty?"

"No. That is not disloyalty."

"Thank you, Jean!" She got up from her chair on the other side of the table and flung herself at him, showering him with kisses. He gently eased her onto his lap, embracing and calming her.

"Theodosia," he asked softly, "did you imagine that you had married a tyrant?"

"No, Jean, but..."

Caressing her hair very softly, he said: "My grandmother taught me to respect people of all faiths and all nationalities and to honor the stranger among us. Did you imagine for one moment that I am like the evil Spaniards who force people to give up their faith and their nationality under torture?"

"But you're making everyone swear fealty to you."

"Only those who wish to serve in my fleet, Theodosia. And only because such suspicion has been cast on multinational crews that if people of two different nations are serving aboard the same ship, the US admiralty courts use this as an excuse to declare that ship forfeit and its flag and the letter of marque that has been issued by me a sham. The only reason I am making my men swear this oath is because I want to establish a legitimate privateering operation that is not open to charges of piracy. And if the Americans even once stopped to think what they are doing, they would realize they are betraying their own principles when they become prejudiced against people from different nations working together in harmony!"

She bowed her head. "Yes, Jean. You are right. And again let me apologize for my country."

"No apology is required, my love."

Chapter Three
Reaping the Whirlwind

She was surprised when Jean announced one day at breakfast: "We have some new neighbors."

"New neighbors?" Jules echoed. "Are there children?"

"Yes, there are whole families. Husbands, wives and children. And they speak French."

"Who are they?" Theodosia asked.

"They are Napoleonic refugees who want to start a new agricultural colony here at Campêche."

"What are Napoleonic refugees, Papa?" Jules asked., throwing a scrap to his dog.

"They are people who have had to leave France because Mr. Bonaparte has been overthrown, and the monarchy has been restored. The Bourbons are now in power again. So the supporters of Mr. Bonaparte have had to flee France and seek refuge here."

"Do you mean like Uncle Arsène?" Jules asked.

"No, Jules. Arsène is an aristocrat."

"But he had to flee France, didn't he? He told me that. He said people were killing people all over the place, that all the French had gone mad, and so he had to leave or they would have chopped his head off."

"Yes. But that was some time ago, Jules. These people are afraid of what the aristocrats who have been restored to power may do to them in revenge for all that head chopping."

60

"Then, do you mean that these are bad people, because they wanted to chop Uncle Arsène's head off?"

"No, Jules. These are just ordinary people who are looking for a place to live."

"So they can go around chopping people's heads off?"

"Oh, for heaven's sakes, Jules," Theodosia exclaimed. "Can you think of nothing but decapitations?"

"They have not come here to chop people's heads off," Jean said patiently. "They have settled here hoping to become farmers. And we need farmers, so we are going to welcome them into our community."

"But how do you know they're not really planning to chop everybody's heads off?" Jules asked. "Once they have gotten settled in?"

"The best way to find out would be to get to know them," Jean said with a smile.

With this encouragement, Jules set out on his own with only the dog at his heels to visit the colonists brought in by General Llalemand. Soon he was spending the majority of each day with his new friends, and Theodosia noticed a marked decline in his English, as he grew more and more immersed in the patois of his new-found friends.

It worried her, not so much because of the fear of decapitation, but because she never saw Jules anymore, except at dinner-time. Sometimes he asked to pack a lunch and insisted on breaking bread with his little comrades in arms.

"It seems very strange that they want to start an agricultural colony here," Theodosia said to Jean one day, when Jules was delayed in returning. "There is hardly any arable land here, is there?"

"Charles Lallemand is no farmer," Jean said. "And he has already had one failure of his Society for the Cultivation of the Vine and Olive."

"Where exactly was he trying to grow olives?" Theodosia asked. "Don't you need a sort of Mediterranean climate for that?"

"He got some land grants in Alabama Territory, and he and his followers settled there last summer. But he spent too much time buying arms and ammunition in New York State and publicizing his plans for the conquest of Texas, so that your Secretary of State, John Quincy Adams, asked him to move his Society for the Cultivation of the Vine and Olive elsewhere. They had nowhere to go, so I let them come here. We do need farmers, Theo, if we are to establish an independent nation."

"I can't stand John Quincy Adams," Theodosia said. "He is not a good man."

"You know him?"

"He is a man who, once you are down, will join the pack of jackals to condemn you. On the last day of 1807, after my father had been found not guilty of treason, but guilty of the misdemeanor of violating the Neutrality Act, John Quincy Adams on the floor of the Senate introduced a motion condemning the 'conspiracy of Aaron Burr against the peace, union and liberties of the people of the United States.' He condemned my father of a crime that the court system had just now found him not guilty of. That's the sort of person John Quincy Adams is."

"Well, I am sorry for that. But the problem is not John Quincy Adams. The real concern is whether these so-called farmers can grow their own food. So far they do not seem to be faring all that well."

It was then that Jules arrived, late for dinner. "I am sorry, Papa," he said. "But I was detained at Champ d'Asile as we had not yet caught any fish."

"Caught any fish?"

"Yes, Papa. My friend Michel is trying to help his family by catching fish, and I was assisting him in this."

"Hadn't he better help them by tending their vine and olives?" Jean asked.

Jules shrugged. "I didn't see any vines or olives, Papa."

"Well, they had better start soon, as the growing season is upon us."

⚹⚹

It was in early April that they had some bad news from Edward Livingston. A letter from the lawyer arrived, in the supply ship from New Orleans, together with a newspaper clipping.

Always eager to read Livingston's chatty, humorous missives, Theodosia waited patiently for Jean to hand it to her. But he dropped the letter on the table and the clipping fell out, and the look of anger in his eyes frightened her.

"What is it, Jean?"

"They hanged John Whitman!"

"What?"

"John Andrew Whitman. They hanged him on March 21st. His lawyers cost me nine thousand dollars!" he said and beat his fist down on the table, sending the dishes clattering.

"His lawyers!"

"Livingston and Grymes! I paid them a fortune to get him off!"

"Was he a close friend of yours, Jean?"

"No, Theodosia, he *worked* for me. He was working for me, and that's why they hanged him."

He stormed out of the room.

Theodosia picked up the clipping that had fallen out from the letter.

New Orleans, March. 1818
On Monday last the awful sentence of the law was executed on Andrew Whitman, who had been convicted before the district court of the state of shooting at one M'Key with intent to commit the crime of murder, an offence which is made capital by statute.

Whitman was a native of Philadelphia, where his connections, though not wealthy, are respectable. From the age of fifteen years, when he first went to sea in a merchant vessel, till he committed the crime for which he suffered death, his life has been a series of perilous adventures and moving accidents by flood and field. He served some time in the American squadron which in the year 1805 humbled the pirates of the Mediterranean; after receiving his discharge, he again betook himself to the merchant service, and was impressed into the British frigate La Virginie; being transferred to another vessel, he soon contrived to effect his escape to the United States. About the year 1812 he joined the piratical establishment at Barrataria, and it was under the banners of John Lafitte that he shot a custom house officer in the execution of his duty. In 1814 he deserted these his worthy associates, and betrayed Pierre Lafitte to the marshal. About this time he enlisted in the 44th

United States regiment of infantry, and was in all the battles which took place during the invasion of Louisiana. Since the peace and subsequent reduction of the army, his career has been extremely vicious; his associates have commonly been the most abandoned villains who fly to New Orleans in order to escape the hand of justice at home; his residence has been in brothels and catalan shops, those sinks of iniquity and receptacles of plunder, where the experienced malefactors may find patrons and coadjutors and the uninitiated are sure to meet with prompters and instructors.

We hope that the example of Whitman will convince the gang of assassins who infest the city of New Orleans, and whose crimes cry aloud to Heaven for punishment, that Justice, though slow, is sure. and will at last assuredly overtake them, although they may triumph in their wickedness and laugh at the idea of detection; above all, we hope it will convince them that the criminal laws of the states are equally just and terrible in their inflictions, and not a mere cobweb to be evaded by the ingenious or prostrated by the powerful.

When Edward Livingston paid them a visit a month later, it was with a heavy heart that he shared with them the last moments of Whitman's life. "Sometimes I think that it would be better to dispense with the death penalty," he said.

"Nonsense," Jean replied. "The death penalty is a bulwark of the law against all manner of rapacious criminality. I use it in my Commune all the time. It is a way to ensure proper obedience and respect from the men. I myself have announced that if any of my men were to molest a married woman, then I will personally hang him from the yardarm of my ship."

"What if he were to molest an unmarried woman?" Theodosia asked.

"There are no unmarried women here at Gálvez Town," Jean said. "It's not allowed."

Seeing Theodosia's stunned expression, Edward Livingston asked, smiling: "You force all the women to get married against their will?"

"Of course not. We don't admit unmarried women. That would cause too much trouble."

"I see." Edward Livingston did not choose to comment further, speaking again only to change the subject. "I have been asked to write a new penal code for the state of Louisiana. I am thinking of leaving the death penalty out of it. Seeing an innocent man hanged has been a very hard lesson for me."

"What would you replace the death penalty with?" Theodosia asked.

"Life imprisonment."

"And it would not break your heart to see an innocent man imprisoned for life?"

"Not as much."

"I would rather be hanged than imprisoned for life," Jean said. "But the error is not in the punishment. The error is in convicting a man who never deserved it. What did they hang him for, shooting at a customs officer who shot first, and missing the man? They might as well hang people for wishing others dead. That's how effective he was against M'Key."

"They hanged him, Jean, as a warning to you."

"He should have been pardoned. Everyone who fought at the Battle of New Orleans was pardoned."

"Yes, Jean," Livingston agreed. "But he switched sides. He was enlisted in the 44th infantry under Ross."

"So he was on *their* side. How could they hang him?"

"Since he was not one of your 'hellish banditti' at the time of the Battle of New Orleans, the pardon did not apply to him."

"Well, that makes no sense. He was with Patterson's raid on Barataria. That should make them happy with him!"

"But they weren't. He had something on Patterson."

"What?"

"I don't know." The lawyer hung his head. "I do not think that Patterson has finished persecuting you, Jean."

"Well, I'm outside his territory now."

"Don't be so sure. Did you read Monroe's first address to Congress last December?"

"Well, of course not. When would I have had time?"

"I happen to have a copy. It mentions you."

"Really? By name?"

"No, not by name."

"Then how do you know it is about me?"

"Shall I read you the relevant portion?"

Jean spread his hands. "How could I stop you?"

Livingston fished up a paper from the pile of documents that the two men had been examining. "First he talks about Amelia Island. Then he mentions Galvez Town."

In the summer of the present year an expedition was set on foot against East Florida by persons claiming to act under the authority of some of the colonies, who took possession of

Amelia Island, at the mouth of the St. Mary's River, near the boundary of the State of Georgia. As this Province lies eastward of the Mississippi, and is bounded by the United States and the ocean on every side, and has been a subject of negotiation with the government of Spain as an indemnity for losses by spoliation or in exchange for territory of equal value westward of the Mississippi, a fact well known to the world, it excited surprise that any countenance should be given to this measure by any of the colonies.

As it would be difficult to reconcile it with the friendly relations existing between the United States and the colonies, a doubt was entertained whether it had been authorized by them, or any of them. This doubt has gained strength by the circumstances which have unfolded themselves in the prosecution of the enterprise, which have marked it as a mere private, unauthorized adventure. Projected and commenced with an incompetent force, reliance seems to have been placed on what might be drawn, in defiance of our laws, from within our limits; and of late, as their resources have failed, it has assumed a more marked character of unfriendliness to us, the island being made a channel for the illicit introduction of slaves from Africa into the United States, an asylum for fugitive slaves from the neighboring states, and a port for smuggling of every kind.

A similar establishment was made at an earlier period by persons of the same description in the Gulf of Mexico at a place called Galvezton, within the limits of the United States, as we contend, under the cession of Louisiana. This enterprise has been marked in a more signal manner by all the objectionable circumstances which characterized the other, and more particularly by the equipment of privateers which have annoyed our commerce, and by smuggling. These establishments, if ever sanctioned by any authority whatever, which is not believed, have abused their trust and forfeited all claim to consideration. A just regard for the rights and interests of the United States required that they should be suppressed, and orders have been accordingly issued to that effect. The imperious considerations which produced this measure will be explained to the parties whom it may in any degree concern.

To obtain correct information on every subject in which the United States are interested; to inspire just sentiments in all persons in authority, on either side, of our friendly disposition so far as it may comport with an impartial neutrality, and to secure proper respect to our commerce in every port and from every flag, it has been thought proper to send a ship of war with three distinguished citizens along the southern coast with these purposes. With the existing authorities, with those in the possession of and exercising the sovereignty, must the communication be held; from them alone can redress for past injuries committed by persons acting under them be

obtained; by them alone can the commission of
the like in future be prevented.

"He cannot mean me," Jean said. "He is probably talking about Aury and Mina."

"I would not be too sure about that, Jean. Patterson is out to get you, and he will not stop until you no longer sail a single ship in the Gulf of Mexico. And Monroe, well, he didn't like Arsène Latour's memoirs. Did you know he suppressed the sale of those books?"

"Why would he do that?"

"Because our friend Arsène did not give him enough credit for winning the Battle of New Orleans."

"What do you mean not enough credit for winning the Battle of New Orleans? He wasn't even there."

Livingston laughed. "Precisely. And how do you think that looked when he was campaigning for president?"

"He was the Secretary of War," Theodosia said. "He could hardly be expected to take the field."

"No. But he sent Andrew Jackson to Florida instead of New Orleans. He saw to it that by the time Jackson's men got to New Orleans, they were out of powder and flints. And any gratitude the nation owes Jean would reflect badly on him."

"Nevertheless, he has sent no one here to evict me," Jean said. "So his report to Congress was erroneous."

"No, he has sent someone," Livingston said solemnly. "But the ways of the government are slow and winding. Whoever it is probably got lost."

At this, they all laughed.

*

"My friend Michel says that nothing will grow here, so General Llalemand tried to move the entire colony inland."

"Yes, Jules, that is true," Jean said. "He rented some pirogues from me for the purpose, but the expedition did not go well, and he sank one of them and drowned its crew. And now they have returned, poorer for the experience."

"Michel said that the Karankawa indians captured some of their men and ate them for dinner."

"Your friend Michel has quite an imagination!" Jean said, his eyes twinkling.

"They're very hungry, Papa."

"The Karankawa?"

"No, Papa. The people of Champ d'Asile are hungry. They have nothing to eat. They only get one biscuit each day and a handful of rice."

"Is that so?"

"Yes, Papa. Don't you think we should give them some food?"

Jean smiled. "I *am* giving them food, Jules. Where do you think that biscuit and the handful of rice have come from? They certainly did not grow it themselves."

"Yes, Papa," Jules said, stuffing some bread into his pockets. "But they are still hungry!"

After the boy had been excused, Theodosia said, "He's feeding his friend, you know."

"Yes, I know."

"Aren't you going to say anything to him about it?"

He shrugged. "What would I say?"

"That he shouldn't give portions of his own meal to strangers?"

"Really?" he asked. "Is that what your father taught you?"

"No, Jean. He gave to everyone generously. Too generously. And now he is bankrupt. I'm afraid..."

"You're afraid that I will go bankrupt supplying these incompetent settlers?"

"How long can you keep sending them food? Isn't it expensive? We're growing nothing here. Everything has to be shipped in."

"We are bringing in rich prizes. Our surplus this year is four hundred thousand, over and above all costs, and after paying each captain and each crewmember and all the expenses of the government. I think we can afford to feed one hundred and twenty settlers until they either learn to thrive on their own or go elsewhere. I won't watch them starve. That would be wrong. I am, after all, responsible for everything that goes on here."

"Do you think it's right for the government to feed the settlers? Won't it result in high taxes for everyone?"

"No. The difference, Theodosia, between what I am doing and the charity they practice in Europe is that *there* they tax farmers to feed soldiers who squander their money. But I make a profit on soldiers so that I can afford to feed farmers."

"I don't understand."

"They tax their own people so they can maintain empires at a loss. I tax those same empires for a profit so I can feed my people."

✳

Pierre came for a visit in July. He brought with him a couple of prizes that had been delayed by customs in New Orleans. He and Marie and the children were now living in a rented house on Rue Royale, for Marie's old house had been sold to make them more mobile and to contribute funds to the Galvez Town project. Pierre recounted his own troubles with Beverly Chew, the Collector of Customs.

"He wrote to Washington, in a open letter, that I had gone back to my piratical ways. Imagine that! Despite the generous pardon that we received."

"Yes, very generous," Jean chuckled. "As long as they kept all our goods for themselves."

"So I wrote back that I was not sorry to help the Mexicans achieve their independence, just as I had been glad to help the United States maintain its own. For without our help, they would surely be a British colony again. And as for that pardon, when was I ever in need of one?"

"What I do not understand is how they fail to doubt the legitimacy of the governments of Britain and Spain, but they doubt ours!" Jean exclaimed. "Why every man under me has chosen to serve of his own free will. Can Spain and Britain say the same of their subjects?"

"But there was no election..." Theodosia said. "So it's not democratic."

"Who needs an election, when you know every man who serves you and have asked him personally if he wishes to do so?" Jean asked.

This seemed so reasonable that Theodosia did not question any further than that.

But Pierre said: "It didn't help Aury much that he held an election on Amelia Island. They still sent the Navy to dispossess him."

"Where they got their idea of legitimacy and authority I will never know," Jean said, wondering. "What was George Washington's authority? Who recognized it until he won the war?"

"The problem is, I still need to do business in New Orleans," Pierre said. "And I need access to the courts. And they're stalling my lawsuit against Gambi."

Theodosia was startled. "You brought a lawsuit against Vincenzo Gambi?"

"Yes. Now *there* is a *real* pirate. Ever since the Battle of New Orleans he has gone rogue. He's attacking all manner of ships, including American vessels."

"And you brought a lawsuit against him for that?"

"No, he's also reneging on all his promises. He owes me $250.00. I gave him plenty of time to pay me back, and at first he said he would, but now he even denies owing it. So finally I decided to sue him. And you know what they're saying?"

"What?"

"That we shouldn't be clogging up the court system with lawsuits between pirates!"

Jean laughed uproariously at this. "Yes, Pierre, why didn't you just ask him to walk the plank?"

⁂

The visit from Antonio de Sedella was unexpected. When she saw him disembarking from the supply ship, Theododia's first instinct was to hide the baby. The second was to restrain Jules, who upon recognizing him, ran happily to greet him.

"Bonjour, Père Antoine!"

The Priest beamed at the little boy. "You have grown so much, Jules!" He never seemed to forget a name, no matter how many parishioners he had to minister to.

"Have you come to join us here at Galvez Town?" the boy asked. "Or perhaps you are going to visit Champ

74

d'Asile?"

"Oh, I plan to visit both establishments," the priest replied suavely. "And who is this?" he said to Theodosia, pointing at the little one in her arms.

"Glenn. Glenn Edward," she muttered.

"Really? What an English-sounding name."

"Maman is English," Jules said to the priest, "and she named him."

"No, Jules. I am not English. I am American."

"But you speak English."

"Yes."

"Why don't you speak American?"

"There is no such language, Jules. Americans speak many different languages. They come from many different places. But they are all American."

"Yes, Maman. Just like the people of Galvez Town."

"Has young Glenn been baptized yet?" de Sedella asked. "For if not, I would be happy to do it."

"He will be baptized when he is old enough to know what it means," Theodosia answered, "and chooses it for himself."

"That is your decision?"

"It is my husband's decision, which I support."

"And where is your husband, Madame?"

"He is on that brig, working on fortifications." She pointed down the sandbar at a beached brig, its masts and spars prominent against the sky.

"What on earth has he grounded that ship there for?"

"It is to protect the settlers of Champ d'Asile."

"I see. More hungry souls for the Church."

She laughed. "They're Protestants fleeing persecution, you know."

"I know," the Priest said, smiling. "But it is never too

late to save a soul from the fires of damnation."

Theodosia felt a chill at those words. She was afraid of de Sedella's power over Jean. After all, that Capuchin friar, who served as a parish priest for all New Orleans and who was once a Holy Inquisitor, controlled the Laffite purse strings. The entire establishment on Snake Island had been built on Spanish gold, and it all came through de Sedella. There were times when Theodosia questioned the priest's loyalty to Spain, as he must have known that Jean's ships regularly preyed on Spanish vessels. But never once did she question his loyalty to the Church.

At dinner, Jean listened patiently to everything de Sedella had to say, until at last the priest ran out of words, and there was a long silence.

Then, in a quiet voice, Jean made his reply: "From our first meetings through the year 1814, I began to note that you acted under a mask. You posed as a pious being with a sensitive heart, but you allowed money to rule you. You revealed yourself and the projects of the Spanish government, hoping that I would lose, little by little, all my confidence and patriotism for the United States, because the United States refused to return my property or offer compensation of any kind. You kept urging me to recruit officers from the New England States, but I could not imagine them adopting the customs of Latin America. You, on the other hand, refused to allow me to recruit officers from the southern states. In the first place, you wanted me to abandon all my commissions as a privateer and to accept the status of a colonial subject of Spain. And in the second place, you now demand that I grant to one religious denomination the right to establish itself in the principal territorial subdivisions. In the third place, you do not have any respect for the Declaration of Independence or the constitution of the United States. In the fourth place, by these stratagems you have no other design than to return all of Louisiana Territory to Spain. Fifthly, I can see now that these subterfuges do not differ materially from the practices employed by your church to shackle all forms of development in good liberal government. Sixthly, I am convinced that you use the word 'independence' for the sole purpose of establishing a powerful religious syndicate with the aim of shackling all progress in the development of liberal thought. In reality, you want nothing better than to see the word 'independence' eradicated from the pages of the dictionary! But that has all come to an end, and you will not succeed in enslaving anyone here!"

There was a stunned silence at the table. Then the priest got up and spoke in a quiet, near whisper, his voice hushed, and yet somehow the sound carried very well: "He who sows the wind will reap the whirlwind! May God have mercy on your soul!" And he got up and left.

Theodosia was so happy that she threw herself into Jean's arm and showered him with kisses. "I am proud of you, Jean! But... can you really afford to cross him?"

He laughed. "He stopped paying me months ago, Theo. The privateering establisment is showing a fine profit. We're on our own now, and we need nothing from anyone."

"But Papa, what if he curses us and makes the sky open up and his god sends a whirlwind against us!"

They both turned and looked at Jules and laughed.

"Jules," Theodosia said. "That only happens in story books."

"Our fortifications can withstand any whirwhind his puny god can muster," Jean added.

☆☆

Having dispensed with the patronage of Spain, they were soon forced to deal with the meddling of the United States. George Graham arrived in what was now known to the Americans as Galvezton on August 24, 1818. He came in a United States Customs boat, courtesy of the Revenue Service.

A charismatic, side-whiskered man-about-town, he first went to speak to General Lallemand at Champ d'Asile.

When he came to call on Jean and Theodosia at La Maison Rouge, he introduced himself as "Colonel George Mason Graham."

"Very nice to meet you," Jean replied. "And what is your business here, sir?"

"I have been sent by the United States government."

Jean was silent for a moment. Then he asked: "In what capacity?"

"Perhaps if you read this letter that I was instructed to deliver to you, all will come clear."

Jean took the letter and breaking the seal in Graham's presence, he started to read it. Theodosia read over his shoulder.

Galvezton August 26, 1818

Mr. J. Laffite

Sir——

I am instructed by the government of the United States to call upon you for an explicit avowal of the national authority, if any, by which you have occupied the position and harbor of Galvezton, and also to make known to you that the government of the United States, claiming the country between the Sabine and the Rio Bravo del Norte, will suffer no establishment of any kind, and more particularly of so questionable a character as that now existing at this place, to be made within these limits without any authority.

I am, with due respect,

Mason Graham

Looking up with a smile from the letter, Jean said: "I will respond immediately." He then turned to Theodosia and asked: "My dear, will you be so kind as to fetch me a pot of ink and pen and paper?" She hurried to get them, and stood behind him and watched as he penned his reply in Graham's presence. She could not help but admire his penmanship and the quick and easy manner with which he composed this short missive. There were not even any misspelled words.

Monsieur—

I will hasten to answer the letter which you did me the honor to write me as soon as you will have the kindness to apprise me of your powers and who authorizes you to put questions of this nature to me.

I have the honor to be

Monsieur

Your obedient servant,

Jn Laffite

Sealing it with his ring on molten wax from the candle that burned on the table, Jean handed the letter to Graham with all due formality, smiling. Graham smiled, too, upon reading it, as if it were all one big joke. Then he drew from the lining of his waistcoat another letter and said: "I am sent here by Mr. John Quincy Adams, who derives his authority from his service in President James Monroe's cabinet as Secretary of State. And here is Mr. Adams' letter authorizing me to act on his behalf in an official capacity under his seal of office."

This time Jean looked at the document for several long moments and his smile vanished. "Very well. I will need some time to reflect and to compose a thorough answer to your questions."

Graham got up, bowed and took his leave.

"Jean, what are you going to do?" Theodosia asked, worried. "There is no way they will accept your authority."

"Why not?" he asked. "Isn't my authority as good as anyone's? Aren't all men created equal?"

"Apparently not," she retorted. "Some men have the good fortune to be close friends with John Quincy Adams. This gives them a great deal more authority than other men, who aren't friends with John Quincy Adams."

He gave her a kiss on the forehead in sign of acknowledgement of her wit. "I will write him a letter," he said. "I will tell the truth. Surely the truth will be enough."

The letter that Jean presented to Graham two days later, whose spelling and grammar had been thoroughly corrected by Theodosia, read as follows:

August 28, 1818

Monsieur—

In answer to the letter which you did me the honor to write to me on the 26th, I will enter into the details of the motives which determined me to occupy the fort at Galvezton.

Mr. Aury was in possession, having been sent here by Minister Erena, as Governor of Galvezton or of Matagorda, by the Mexican Congress. The instability of his character decided him to abandon this post, during the invasion of the traitor Mina, with no need which was beginning to be of some consequence, and would, not doubt, become of the greatest importance.

I was at Galvezton at the moment of abandonment. I conceived the idea of preserving and maintaining it at my own expense. No one disputed my possession. I satisfied two passions that dominated me; one, to offer a refuge to the armed vessels of the Party of Independence, and the other, to be able, because of its proximity, to rush to the aid of the United States, if circumstances required. Satisfied with the sincerity of my motives, I boldly put this plan into execution.

I declare that the strictest orders were given not only to respect the

American flag, and also to go to its aid on all occasions and always with disinterestedness which manifests the purity of my intentions. I will not add more to this subject, of which chance has made you a witness.

I have written several times to the Mexican Congress to obtain the legitimate sanction of my taking possession and the naming of the authorities and other municipal officers for the organization of a regular and legitimate government, but the circumstances of the existing war having forced Congress to abandon the place of its sittings and to hold them at too great a distance from the seacoast, it became impossible for my letters to reach their destination.

I was then ignorant of the fact that the American government had the intention to claim all the coast from the Sabine to the Rio Bravo. My conduct has been frank and loyal, and, whatever may be the fate reserved for me, I would appreciate your giving to the Government the assurance of my obedience and my entire resignation to its will.

I know, sir, that I have been calumniated in the vilest manner by persons invested with a certain importance, but, fortified by a conscience which is irreproachable in every way, my internal tranquillity has not been affected and, in spite of my enemies, I shall obtain (no doubt sooner or later) the justice which is due me.

I have the honor to be, with high consideration,

Monsieur

Your very humble

And very obedient servant

Jn̲ Laffite

During Graham's two week stay, Jean endeavored to show him a very good time, including hunting and fishing and many dinners with the best of victuals. While Graham could promise nothing, he did seem to warm to Jean and even offered to inquire in New Orleans of the consul of the Republic of Buenos Aires, with whom the United States was then on good relations, whether authority for the Galvezton admiralty court might be obtained through Buenos Aires.

And then George Graham departed on the Revenue Cutter, and with him went high hopes for the future. But no sooner had the envoy from Washington gone, but a great wind arose from the sea, and gusts of a hundred miles an hour or more smashed into Campêche.

It happened very suddenly. One moment all seemed calm, and then everything was in a flurry.

"All women and children to La Maison Rouge!" the cry was raised.

And all the men set out on board the ships.

Theodosia huddled under the great table in the Red House with Glenn and Jules close beside her. Many of the women of Champ d'Asile were praying to an angry god, amid the creaking timbers, and crying babies.

Just before the rafters fell in on them, Jules asked: "Maman, do you think this is the whirlwind that Père Antoine was speaking of?"

Chapter Four
Of Cannibals and Pirates

When Theodosia awoke, she was buried under a beam, partially immersed in water and a hand was reaching out to touch her. "Jean?" she mumbled, but it was not Jean. It was not even a speaker of English or French or Spanish. There were several men working on unearthing the women and children from the debris, and they spoke a language Theodosia had never heard before.

The baby was unharmed. He started to cry, and she placed him at her breast, for her hands were not pinned down, and there was a hollow space between the beams and themselves. The water on the floor was shallow, and she had no trouble keeping her upper torso above it. "Jules?" she called.

"I'm here, Maman," she heard him say. "I am helping the cannibals get you out."

"What cannibals?"

"The ones who ate those settlers, Maman. They are called Karankawa. It's all right, though, because they don't eat dogs. Their name means dog lovers. So Bandito is safe."

The dog's name had undergone a subtle transformation since Jean gave that puppy to Jules. First he had been called Benedito, as Jules had hoped the Père Antoine would baptise the puppy and offer it everlasting life. When the priest refused, the name became Bandito, like one of those hellish banditti that Governor Claiborne had complained of.

"Well, if Bandito is safe," Theodosia sighed, "then eveything must be all right."

Once she had been released from under the pile of rubble, Theodosia found that her bones were all intact, her clothing slightly torn and her skirt soaking wet, her arms and legs somewhat scratched up, but she was not in need of medical assistance. Some of the other women had not been as lucky. Two were dead. Several more were badly injured.

All who survived stood staring at their rescuers, who were about thirty men, stark naked, over six feet tall, covered with colorful tattoos in geometric shapes, their lower lips and nipples pierced through with small pieces of wood. They placed the rescued women and their children in their dugout canoes, and made for an area further inland which had not been flooded.

"Maman, do you think they want to eat us?" Jules asked, tugging at her torn skirt, Bandito curled up at his feet.

"I don't think so, Jules," she replied as calmly as she could. Clutching Glenn Edward tightly to her breast, she was trying not to stare at the man paddling the canoe. She did not know where to look, and she remembered being told by her father that when treating with the natives, one should never gape, but show the greatest of respect, no matter how outlandish their attire. She decided the best thing to do was to lower her gaze, the way she had seen the slave women on Joseph's plantation do whenever a white man approached them.

But some of the other rescued women became hysterical when carried out of the rubble in the arms of what they perceived as a savage, and several fainted and had to be revived. One woman insisted in French, in a loud shrill voice, that these were the very men who had eaten her husband when he was yet alive several months earlier.

"Madame Lalouche, *silence!*" some of the more discreet matrons of Champ d'Asile called out to her.

Galvez Town had been devastated by the storm. Snake Island was flooded about four foot deep. Almost all the buildings had been damaged beyond repair, with only six left standing. All the ships that had remained docked had had their spars and masts shattered and their hull damaged and battered.

Bandito whined, his head now on Jules' lap. The rower stopped in mid-stroke and petted the dog, who immediately quieted down, his tail wagging.

"They must be good people," Jules said. "If they like dogs."

"Yes, Jules," she answered. It was best to hold on to hopeful thoughts, though she was not unaware of the fact that some people were known to be kind to dumb animals while very cruel to their fellow man.

Their destination was a series of thatched huts, on the banks of the Trinity river some distance inland. They were handed over to the women of the tribe, who offered them dry blankets while their wet clothes were drying and served them a meal of fried fish.

One of the Karankawa women spoke some French. She approached Theodosia and said: "Vous ête la femme de Laffite?"

Theodosia nodded.

The young woman told her in halting French that she had once worked for her husband and that no harm would come to them, as they had an arrangement with the chieftain at Campêche concerning hunting and fishing rights on the island.

"*Et vous ne mangez pas des hommes?*" Jules asked.

The girl smiled, a glint in her eye. "*Seulement des mechants hommes,*" she said modestly.

"You see, Maman," he told her after. "There is nothing to worry about. They only eat *bad* people."

Theodosia laughed. "Well, that is a comfort, Jules."

But others did not find this assurance quite as comforting. Later in the day, Madame Lalouche found a musket in one of the huts and threatened to shoot, pointing wildly in the direction of the native women.

Theodosia stepped up to her and said: "Put it down, Madame. They are helping us. You will get us all killed if you don't stop."

"You heard what they said. They do eat people. They ate my Jacques."

"I'm sure they didn't."

"We found his fingers afterwards," Madame Lalouche insisted. "The very tips of his fingers. By the river. They're going to eat us all!"

"Jules, could you go get that girl who speaks French," Theodosia said to him, while striding up to Madame Lalouche.

"Yes, Maman." The boy ran off, followed by the dog.

Theodosia put her hand on the butt of the gun and was reaching for the barrel. Madame Lalouche tried to fire, but nothing happened. It was then that she let her fingers be pried off the trigger, and Theodosia returned the gun to one of the native women, who had been watching. "I'm sorry," she said, and the woman inclined her head, as if she had understood.

Jules came back with the interpreter. When Jules explained Madame Lalouche's complaint, the young girl laughed. "It was not *we* who ate your husband, Madame. It was an alligator."

⁂

The water on Snake Island slowly receded, the ships that had gone out in the storm came back, and a few of them were still in excellent condition. The *Jupiter* was damaged, but the *General Victoria* became Jean's personal headquarters, and where his family was housed. During the process of rebuilding La Maison Rouge and the storehouses and homes on the shore, two ships were used as government offices and as a temporary replacement for the great red house that had been destroyed: the *Ciel Bleu* and the *Saragossa*. The latter was headquarters for all formal bookkeeping, banking and the processing of prizes. "It is a sort of Customs House," Jean explained to Theodosia. "Only the difference between our customs and theirs is this: that *they* take money from merchants and increase the price of goods for ordinary people so that they can pay their armies, while we tax our military who live off our enemies so as to leave some money to feed the people."

"So, what you are really saying, Papa," Jules interrupted, "is that we are cannibals, like the Karankawa."

"No, Jules, we are not cannibals," Jean replied quite seriously, "and neither are the Karankawa."

"But they eat people. They admitted it themselves. And you just said that we feed off our enemies."

"They do not eat people for food, son. They only sometimes feast on captured enemies in order to gain their spirit magic."

Theodosia looked at him. He sounded perfectly serious. "Jean, you can't mean that you think it is all right to eat people for their spirit magic?"

He laughed. "It is not a practice that I advocate, my

love, but it not cannibalism."

"Why not? They eat people."

"Not their *own* people. And not people they do business with. They only ever do it as a warning to enemies, and never for food."

"So cannibals are only those who eat their own people, Papa?"

"Yes, Jules. All people eat something. Everything we eat is living. But we are not cannibals unless we eat each other."

"Then Glenn is a cannibal," Jules cried in delight, "because all he ever eats is Maman!"

"Jules!"

"Well, he does. I have never seen him eat anything else."

Jean took a sideways glance at Theodosia. "I think maybe you should let him try some solid food."

"Yes, Jean. But there isn't enough to eat right now."

He looked uncomfortable. "Well, that supply ship is due in any time."

"So we're not cannibals because we feed on our enemies and not our friends?" Jules asked.

"Yes."

"Because we only eat *bad* people?"

"Jules!" Theodosia remonstated.

"*Oui, mon fils,*" Jean replied. "Only very bad people."

Chapter Five
The Panic Begins

There was not much food left before the supply ship pulled into Galvez port in late October of 1818. Everyone was now on rations, not just the people of Champ d'Asile. The Karankawa, who had helped to rebuild some of the town and who had saved the women from the collapsed building, had taken as payment not only muskets and flints, but also a considerable portion of their remaining supplies.

General Lallemand had departed with George Graham back in September before the storm, and he had not returned, leaving his followers to fend for themselves. They were starving.

Theodosia worried about Jules. As long as Glenn was not yet weaned, he had enough to eat. But Jules was an active boy, and she thought she saw him growing thin before her very eyes.

Often he would pocket his food in a kerchief without eating it and go to share the meal with his friend Michel. Theodosia suspected that the other boy ate more of Jules' meal than Jules did. Even the dog, Bandito, seemed shortchanged by the deal, and he whined sadly under the table.

"I think we should forbid him to go there," she said to Jean.

"I will not forbid it."

"Why not?"

"It's his food. He may share it, if he wishes."

"But it will weaken him."

"He is strong enough."

She thought about Gampy and how she had lost him to malaria. Seeing Jules lose weight frightened her. "But isn't it our duty to see to it that he is as strong as he can be?"

"It is our duty to let him grow strong in his own way."

"General Lallemand has abandoned his people," Jules said, when he returned one day from his friend's house. "So I have decided to give Michel all my meals."

"Really?" Jean asked, with one eyebrow arched.

"Yes." Jules sounded very brave, but Theodosia also felt somehow that he was testing them.

"All your food?" Jean asked.

"Yes, Papa, because he needs it more."

"You mean that he needs to live more than you do?"

"No, Papa. But I have more."

"More what?"

"More strength."

After about two days, Jules no longer had more strength. He was slow and dispirited.

"We have to give him something to eat," Theodosia said to Jean.

"We *are* giving him something to eat," Jean replied. "Three times a day."

"But..."

"When he is hungry enough, he will eat."

On the third day, Jules resumed eating his meals with the family.

"You're not donating all your food to Michel?" Jean

asked with a smile.

"No, Papa. I have to eat, too. But I will bring him my scraps, after Bandito has eaten first."

"That is a good policy," Jean said. "Bandito has been looking a little scrawny lately."

Theodosia sighed in relief.

.

⚘

"We found a stowaway aboard the supply ship," James Campbell announced Two sailors brought the man, in irons before Jean in his office on the *Saragossa*.

"What is your name?"

"Francis Little."

Theodosia, who was seated to the left of Jean, looked at the man with curiosity. He was rather a short fellow, with a wiry frame and tousled blond mane. His blue eyes were set wide apart, which she took for a sign of intelligence, and the way the corners of his mouth turned up just a little made her sure he was not a hardened ruffian. He was really not much more than a boy. Theodosia felt a sudden ache in her heart, as the thought raced through her mind, completely unbidden: "That could have been my son."

Of course, the thought was ridiculous. Gampy would not have looked like that. Gampy was not blond. Gampy had dark brown eyes, almost black in their darkness. He had the eyes of Aaron Burr, almost too large for his face. But this boy sported eyes that were slanted and narrow and almost slitted against the light, and the blond lashes that framed them did little to widen their gaze. Gampy had been a scholar, but this young man, by the look of him, was an artisan. Theodosia played such games with herself when looking at people's faces. She was often wrong in her judgments, but it did not deter her. "Gampy would have been almost seventeen," she thought to herself. "If he were alive today."

"Why did you board the vessel without permission?"

"I didn't have fare for the passage."

"Why didn't you sign up for the crew?" Jean asked.

"I tried. They chose others over me."

"Are you a sailor?"

"No, Sir."

"Have you a trade?"

"Yes, Sir. I'm a carpenter."

"Apprenticed?"

"I completed my apprenticeship, Sir. I was apprenticed at fourteen. I am now a master."

"And couldn't you find work?"

"No, Sir, I looked everywhere. There are no jobs for carpenters now. No jobs at all."

"How can that be?"

"They're not hiring, Sir. The money is tight."

"Since when?"

"Since last month."

Jean looked to Campbell for confirmation. "Is that true, James?"

"Yes, Jean. The Second Bank of the United States called in its loans, because the government needed the principal so it could make the payment on Louisiana Territory that was due to Napoleon."

Jean laughed. "Is that so, James? They sent him the payment to the Island of St. Helena, did they?"

Campbell looked a little confused. "Er, well, that's what I read in the papers."

Theodosia spoke up. "You know perfectly well that Napoleon assigned those notes from Jefferson to an English

94

bank, Jean."

He smiled. "Is that what you heard, too, Mr. Little?"

The boy looked down. "I don't know much about high finance, Sir. I just know there are no jobs, because money is tight."

"Then why did you board the ship?"

"Because I heard *you* were hiring, Sir."

"You did?"

"Yes, Sir, they said what with the hurricane knocking down your establishment, you had work for a carpenter or two."

"Indeed," Jean replied. "I have enough work for four carpenters and a master blacksmith."

"Have you filled all the positions, Sir?"

"I have now!" Jean replied smiling. "You will work off your fare, after which you will be paid the advertised wages for the remainder of your work."

"Yes, Sir."

As the boy was released, Theodosia asked Jean: "Is it true? Is money that tight in the States?"

"Apparently so. You know that the banks were issuing so much paper currency with so little cover during the war, that specie payments were always scarce. If they had been able to repay their debts from booty gotten from the British upon winning the war, all could have been set right. But the British gave them nothing in return for the peace, and now the country is bankrupt and owes that money to the British."

"Is there anything we can do about this?" she asked.

"I have to spend some time rebuilding my fort on the Trinity River that was knocked down during the storm. It is forty-five kilometers from here, so it will require a protracted absence. When that work is done, I will set out to meet with John Quincy Adams in Washington City to discuss George Graham's visit."

"Jean, John Quincy Adams will do nothing for you."

"Yes, but *I* might be able to do something for *him*," he answered, smiling.

⁂

Jean took Francis Little with him to work on the fort, and when he returned, he had so much trust in young Frank, as he took to calling him, that he decided to take the boy with him on his trip east, to see the Secretary of State. In his absence, Jean de la Porte and Herman Gramonton were on duty, in charge of the Admiralty Court and the Customs House.

"I don't like it," James Campbell complained to Theodosia. "They've gone lax. They are handing out letters of marque with Jean's signature on them to every Tom, Dick and Harry. "

"What do you mean?"

"Jean always screens the men, makes sure they're decent. But now they are handing out letters of marque to known pirates."

"Known pirates?"

"That's right. There's a whole mess of them who work for Gambi. They prey on anything with sails, and they are rough on the passengers and put their hands on the women. Jean would never stand for that. But some of those men have been given letters of marque right under our noses."

"Who?" Theodosia asked.

"Francis Neely, George Brown, Jean Marotte, the whole lot of them crooks and robbers. Gambi's followers, every one."

"You will tell Jean, when he gets back?"

"Of course, but it may be too late. There is no telling what mischief they will do, using those letters of marque. In Jean's name, no less!"

✣

"John Quincy Adams is about fifty years old, balding, round pated. He received me and treated me with much consideration."

"I doubt that," Theodosia interjected.

"You may doubt, but it is true. He declared that he has never authorized Mr. Graham to investigate in Galvez Town."

"Seriously!" Theodosia jumped up. "But Jean, we saw the document with Adams' signature, and his seal of office! Are we expected to believe that it was forged?"

"Calm down, my dear. You would never make a diplomat with that fire in you. It does not matter. When he met with me, he disavowed all knowledge of it."

"Well, that shows that he's a liar. A cunning, fraudulent liar!"

"Do you want me to tell you what happened, or do you just want to cast aspersions against your most noble Secretary of State?" Jean asked. "As I recall, you are still an American citizen."

"As I recall," she replied. "American citizens are entitled to do just that. But... all right, tell me what happened."

"Well, I went straight to John Quincy Adams as soon as I arrived in Washington. He was amiable. He was kind. He offered me sherry."

"And you declined?"

"Of course. I suggested we should have some coffee,

instead."

"And did you?"

"No. He said coffee disagrees with him."

"Ah. That figures!"

"He said he never authorized Graham to come here, and that as far as he was concerned, Mr. Graham was working for himself and himself alone. He had no authorization from any member of the United States government to expel us from Galvez Town."

"Really? So James Monroe, in his first address to Congress in December of 1817 did not say that he was sending someone to ask the establishment at Galvezton to disband?"

Jean laughed. "Well, it could not have been Graham he was sending, as that would mean the trip had taken him eight months."

"Oh, he probably sent him to Florida first."

"Mr. Adams told me that Mr. Graham was in the banking business and was interested in loans and credits to private concerns."

"It seems to me that not only Mr. Graham, but also the Federal goverment is in the banking business and is interested in loans and credits to private concerns," said Theodosia. "Or what is the Second Bank of the United States for?"

"I mentioned Thomas Jefferson," Jean said.

"You didn't!?"

"Yes, I mentioned him and Napoleon both."

She laughed. "Not in the same breath, surely?"

"And the Louisiana Purchase, and those promissory notes. Those pesky little bank notes that came due this summer."

"No! What did Mr. Adams say to that?"

"He said that Mr. Graham did not like the ideas of Thomas Jefferson nor the system of Napoleon."

"Jean, you do realize he was speaking about himself, not Mr. Graham?"

"The thought did cross my mind."

"So how then did your interview conclude?"

"I told Mr. Adams about the reports I have had from my spies about the English agents and their attempts at subversion. I showed him maps of where they were trying to stir up the native tribes against the Americans. I let him understand that the peace with Britain is a sham, and how it would be very shameful for the United States to bankrupt themselves in an attempt to pay tribute to the British Crown. Because the debt to pay for Louisiana Territory is no longer a debt to France, and there is no reason to pay it to Britain when we won the war against them. They should be paying the United States, instead. I told him that if only he gave the word, we could get a regular income for the United States in the sum of $400,000.00 every month, by attacking the British shipping lanes."

"And what did he say to that?"

"He said he was a great friend of Britain."

She laughed. "That's true. He is. He always was. As was his father before him."

"I told him that those who prey on their own people are cannibals. And this is what he is doing to appease England and weaken the life blood of his own nation." Jean sighed. "I failed in my mission in Washington."

Then one day in late December, Denise appeared out

of nowhere. Francis Neely brought in a prize to process, and when he swaggered into the *Saragossa's* offices to present the papers to Jean, Denise was on his arm, dressed in a stylish, sparkling new gown.

Jean got up from his chair, flustered. "Denise, what are you doing here?"

"Papa, allow me to introduce my new husband, Captain Francis Neely."

He stared at her with a gaping mouth.

"But, of course, you know him. You must, because you signed his letter of marque."

"Denise, I told you to remain in New Orleans."

"Yes, Papa. You said I was not to come, because it is unsafe for an unmarried woman to go unescorted on Snake Island. But now I am married. So all is well!"

Chapter Six
A Daughter of El Cid

"We must have the marriage annulled!"

"No, Jean, you cannot do that!" Yvonne jumped up and blocked his way.

He had called a family conference. Everyone was there, for it was the holiday season, and those members from far away had come into Galvez Town. Yvonne and Laurent Maire whose ship had just docked, Marie and Pierre who had come in from New Orleans, and even Antoine, his elder son, who was visiting from the East. Everyone had some advice to offer. Everyone felt free to say what they thought. Only Theodosia sat huddled in the corner of the stateroom, afraid to venture an opinion. She felt very small and useless and not a little guilty.

In the past two years, Denise had hardly crossed her mind. She had known at the outset that leaving a young girl behind alone in a big city, walled up in a convent school, and open to the machinations of the Spanish priest who was pulling the strings of all the local politicians, was wrong. She had tried to tell Jean, and Jean had curtly reminded her that Denise was not her daughter. This statement of ownership, of right and title, had silenced her. Denise had begged her to intervene on her behalf, and Theodosia had done nothing.

All her moral strength had gone into standing up to

Jean on the issue of James Wilkinson. The man who had betrayed her father and perjured himself to incriminate him was at the time Jean's boss. Together they were spying for Spain against the United States. That Jean had taken Spanish gold Theodosia could accept, under the circumstances after the Battle of New Orleans with the treachery of Madison's adminstration toward him. But that he was working for James Wilkinson, who had ruined her father and may well have had Merriwether Lewis assassinated to keep Jefferson from knowing the truth, this she could not stomach! So she wagered everything on her ability to move Jean to abandon Wilkinson, and when she lost, her faith in herself was shattered.

What really did she have to offer Jean? Only her own body, her mind and her soul. He had taken it all and laughed in her face. He had impregnated her with Glenn upon his return from the mapping expedition, then told her that if she could not bear to live with a man who worked for James Wilkinson, he was willing to dissolve their partnership. Where would she have gone? Back to her father's one room in a shabby, lice-ridden boarding house in New York City, with two bastards to feed? What choice did she have but to stay with him?

No, that wasn't right. It was not the only reason she had stayed. She would have died of loneliness to be forever parted from him. She could not bear it, and that is why she submitted to him like a clockwork doll whenever he had need of her, and the dockworkers could set their watches by her pleasure cry. For their marriage, though a happy one, had become rather predictable of late.

"No wife worth her salt ever abides by her husband's decision about anything!" Denise had declared, when Theodosia refused to intervene on her behalf.

It was true. Other wives had some kind of magical power over their husbands, a power Theodosia was not endowed with. How could she deny him anything, without denying herself? Was the secret weapon of the average wife that she did not really love her husband?

Yet, she had promised to serve him faithfully, and when she did not speak up for Denise, who was the apple of his eye, had she not betrayed that trust?

"Why shouldn't I annul the marriage?" Jean asked. "She is underage. She is too young to be married. And I never gave my consent."

"And what if he has gotten her with child?" Yvonne asked reasonably. "Do you want that child to be a bastard?"

He paused for a moment, and the look on his face was torture. "I don't want him touching her," he said softly.

"It's too late for that, Jean," Pierre said, putting his hand on his shoulder. "That ship has already sailed."

The door to the stateroom flew open, and Denise marched in. "I heard there was a family meeting called," she said. "Did you forget to invite me, Papa?"

"Denise..."

"I see everyone is here. Well, what are we discussing? The depressed economy perhaps? Or the exchange rate for Spanish doubloons?"

"No, Denise. It is your happiness that we are concerned with," Yvonne said.

"Well, I am very happy, as all newly wed wives ought to be."

Jean approached her and with a very serious, quiet voice he asked: "Denise, do you feel affection for that man, Francis Neely?"

"No, Papa, but then affection is not a sufficient basis for marriage, nor is it required."

"Who told you that?"

"Why Emma did. When the two of you were engaged to be married, and I questioned her motives."

Everyone turned to look at Theodosia. She could feel her cheeks growing red.

"What do you mean?" Jean asked woodenly.

For a moment, Denise closed her eyes, as if scanning a page in her mind. Then she opened them wide and declaimed: "'I have no affection for your father, as you do. Nor has he any for me, as he does for you. He uses me mercilessly, and I will gladly send him out to war, even if it means his death, and I believe that there are things far more important than affection between a man and a woman.' You said that, didn't you, Emma?"

Theodosia was speechless. It sounded like her words, though she did not remember saying exactly that. What had Denise done? Had she written it down immediately after so as to use it as ammunition against her stepmother years later?

Jean looked at Theodosia for one sharp painful moment without comment, but directed his gaze right back at Denise. "If you have no affection for him," he said, "it is not too late. We can have the marriage annulled."

"No, Papa. Francis uses me as any proper husband would, and I adore him for that. Affection would only sully our passion. And as I see I am not welcome here at this family meeting, I will return to my husband's ship. We sail at dawn. I hope to win many prizes for you, Papa!"

"Denise!"

She ran out of the cabin, but a moment later she came scurrying back, and walked right up to Jean and standing on tiptoes, she planted a kiss on his cheek. "I still love you, Papa!"

And then she was gone.

⚹

When they were finally alone that night, with Jules asleep on his narrow cot and Bandito at his feet and Glenn curled up in the basket that used to serve Jules for a crib, Theodosia had expected recriminations. But Jean did not mention Denise or the words she had quoted against her.

"Jean, I'm sorry. I failed you. I should have fought for Denise to be allowed to come with us to Snake Island."

"Why?"

"Because I knew it was not safe to leave her there in New Orleans. I should have alerted you to this problem. It was my fault. I'm sorry."

"No need to apologize. It would have made no difference. I would never have listened to you."

There was not an ounce of real warmth in his absolution. It was more like a cold slap in the face.

"Jean..."

"I'm tired," he said and put out the lamp.

⚹

Edward Livingston came for a visit in February of 1819. As usual, he brought with him piles of legal documents for Jean to sign and newspaper clippings that he thought were of particular interest concerning the latest events.

"The good news," said Livingston smiling, "is that the United States has given up its claims to all territory west of the Sabine River. The bad news is that we just gave it all to Spain in the Adams-Onis Treaty. "

"They cannot give something they never owned in the first place to Spain or anyone else."

"Yes, well, you did claim it for Spain in the first place, didn't you, Jean?"

"No, Ed. I was using Spanish gold, but I claimed it for the Mexican revolutionaries. In this, of course, I had de Sedella's blessing. I helped Aury and Mina claim Galvez Town for the Mexican Congress. But since that revolution has failed, and there is no Republic of Mexico and no Mexican congress, I am currently holding it in trust for Cartagena."

"Well, that is most kind of you," Livingston chuckled. "But just so you know, Onis thinks he bought all of Texas from Adams for a nickel and a dime."

"That's probably why that old codger in Washington told me he had not authorized Graham to claim my property for the United States. Because it would have been embarrassing to admit he had changed his mind and does not want it, anymore. He probably would not be able to pay the upkeep on it. He seemed a little low on funds."

"The country is going to hell in a handbasket," Livingston said, spreading the papers out on the table. "Everyone is in debt, and the debts are past due. The rich are debtors, the poor are debtors, farmers are debtors, the banks are debtors, the great manufacturing interests are debtors. Debtors outnumber creditors ten to one, and they can't repay. And because of this, those people who are owed the money are afraid to raise a hue and cry to demand the restoration of specie payments at once. Since the creditors are in the minority, both among the rich and the poor, they would be drawn and quartered as traitors to society if they called in the amounts due them. That's how they are getting away with suspending specie payments."

"You mean, they've closed all the banks?" Jean asked.

"On the contrary. They have allowed the banks to continue in business while suspending payments in specie."

"Why, that's preposterous! All the banks?"

"Not all of them yet. They are going state by state, passing three different kinds of laws through the legislature that make it impossible to conduct regular business."

"Three kinds of laws?" Theodosia asked. "What do you mean?"

"They are called stay laws, minimum appraisal laws and compulsory par laws. Stay laws impose a moratorium on the collection of debts. Minimum appraisal laws set a fixed price below which a debtor's goods cannot be sold at auction."

"And compulsory par laws do what?"

"They prohibit one from exchanging bank notes at a discount."

"But how can that possibly work?"

"It doesn't. Many people are going back to the barter system. Out in the western territories, *whisky* is the favored medium of exchange."

Jean laughed. "Yes, I can see how that would work."

"So how are things here?" Livingston gave him a sharp glance.

"We still use silver and gold."

"That's not what I meant, Jean. I heard about Denise's elopement."

He sighed. "Yes. Well. I suppose everyone has heard of it."

"Are you going to have it annulled?"

"No, Ed. What would be the point?"

"You know, it's de Sedella's doing."

"That she fell in love?"

"He... encouraged it."

"How could he do that?"

"He introduced them. I've had the matter investigated, in case you wanted to act on it. De Sedella gave Neely leave to visit her in the convent. And then, when they tumbled into each others' arms, he spoke of the fires of hell."

Jean laughed. "Denise is not afraid of the fires of hell. I sometimes almost wish she were."

"No, but they were married in the Catholic Church."

"In that case, Ed, were there no banns of marriage published? Why didn't you warn me?"

"There were, Jean. I didn't know at the time that you had not approved it. I'm sorry."

Livingston looked over at Theodosia who was feeding Glenn some oatmeal in the corner of the room. She did not meet his glance. She had been in trouble with Jean for two months now, and she was miserable. When the talk was not of high finance or legal matters, she no longer dared to utter a word.

But Jean was not entirely forthcoming when he answered the lawyer's question. Things were not going well at Galvez Town, either. The problems here were not financial. They were with the quality of captains who had recently been given letters of marque in Jean's absence; several turned out to be rogue operators and out-and-out pirates. Whenever a new act of piracy turned up, a trial was convened, and upon conviction the guilty party was summarily hanged. There were three sitting judges and panels of thirteen jurors at the ready for each new offense. Which is why when Edward Livingston had disembarked that day, he saw two fresh bodies hanging from the yardarms of the *Saragossa*. But Livingston was very discreet and did not inquire any further.

⁂

In late February, Jean made a short trip to New Orleans. "A good friend of mine is need of money, and I am going to loan him $4,800.00," Jean told Theodosia.

"Do you think that is wise, Jean? Creditors are outnumbered ten to one, remember?"

"I think I can rely on repayment," he said laughing. "My friends know me well, and they realize I will not be trifled with. Also, I plan to help Marie repurchase her old house at the corner of Rue Bourbon and Rue Philip."

She did not say a thing. But Jean could read her thoughts.

"She sold the house to help Pierre put in his share of the investment in the privateering venture in Galvez Town. We promised her that as soon as we were showing a profit, she would have her house back. I always keep my promises."

"Yes, Jean."

"Anyway, this is a fine time to buy, for those who have the cash. I am making a very good deal with Antoine Abat, $9000.00 in four equal payments."

"That's a lot of money." She would have liked to own a house in New Orleans, but did not say so. She did not own anything. She had never had anything of her own, even though she had been a vice president's daughter. Marie Villard was the granddaughter of a freed slave, and yet she was now a member of the landowning class.

"It depends on who you are, how much money nine thousand dollars are," Jean replied. "A common laborer earns one dollar a day on average. So it would take him twenty-seven years to amass that sum, more or less. But Pierre and I have a $476,000.00 surplus, and so it is a small matter for us to buy that house for Marie."

Marie Villard was not married to Pierre, but she had a contract of plaçage which guaranteed her that she would be the owner of a house and that her children would be acknowledged and provided for. Jean and Pierre took every contract they signed very seriously, and so Marie's position was guaranteed.

Theodosia had no contract. All she had was the promise that he would go with her all the way to hell if necessary. But what exactly did that mean? What was the value of this promise in dollars and cents? She could demand nothing, and of late, with Jean spurning her over her misguided declaration of non-affection six years ago, she was feeling very insecure. She no longer dared to mention Denise.

It did not help that there were rumors. "El Commandante has been seen dining out with a quadroon." She heard the things whispered among the dockworkers and the sailors and the shopkeepers of Galvez Town.

"I was in New Orleans not a fortnight ago, and Jean Laffite had with him a young girl barely out of childhood, her eyes big and round and dark as night." This from a New Orleans merchant passing through town.

"Laffite the younger has taken a mulatto mistress. She is the sister of Marie Villard, who is the mistress of his brother. And they all live together in the same house. They share everything." Followed by laughter.

She tried to disregard the stories in his absence, but when he returned, it became much harder. She was sure he had changed. His feelings toward her had changed. There were no more pleasure cries in the night, and during the day he spoke to her only of business.

"Many Americans are very bitter about the sale of

Texas to Spain," he told her. "Some have sworn to claim the land west of the Sabine for themselves, treaty or no treaty. There are some American settlers at Natchez who are just waiting for a fight."

"But don't they know that we're already here?" Theodosia asked. "And that you have sovereignty over this land?"

"Apparently they consider us a natural part of the landscape, just like the Karankawa, to be sold to the highest bidder."

"Did you hear news of Francis Neely?" Theodosia asked., not looking at him.

He shrugged.

"You heard nothing?"

"Only rumors. I heard he was attacking American vessels. But let us hope it is not true, for then I will have to hang him."

Then one night the unthinkable happened. A sloop came alongside the *General Victoria,* and a cargo was dumped on the dock. Then the sloop stole away.

It was Bandito who noticed and raised the alarm. He kept barking and asking to be let out, and finally Jean had no choice but to go out with the dog, because it refused to go without him.

That's how he found her lying like a sack of flour on the dock, naked, and almost lifeless and bound. He turned her over to see her face, and only then did he know. "Denise!"

There was no time for talking. He brought her in and laid her on the bed, and said: "I am going to fetch a doctor!"

"But Jean, you're an alchemist. Can't you help her?"

He gave her a disdainful look, as if she were a fool. "She is my daughter, and I am going to fetch a doctor."

He had not gotten a doctor to help with her childbirth. Not the first time, when she nearly died, nor the second time, which had been easier, but still very hard. He had pretended to be such a great medical expert. And yet now that his daughter's life lay in the balance, he was going to move heaven and earth to find a doctor!

"But what will you tell the doctor?" she called after him.

"Yellow fever," he said between gritted teeth. "I will say she has yellow fever. Or typhoid. Or malaria."

⚜

Doctor Felix Formento was an Italian physician who ministered to the Champ d'Asile settlement. Like all doctors, he asked for water to be boiled as soon as he arrived, although as far as Theodosia was able to observe, the only thing he used the boiled water for was to wash his hands and arms up to the elbow.

After examining Denise thoroughly, he summoned Jean and stated in a quiet voice with a slight accusatory tone: "She does not have yellow fever, nor typhoid, nor cholera, nor malaria. Nor any of the other diseases you mentioned when you summoned me, Monsieur Laffite. What have you done to her?"

"She is my daughter. I have done nothing. What is wrong with her? Was she beaten?"

"No. Her injuries are internal. She is suffering from shock. The womb has been exposed to too much seed. It causes contractions, and can end in sepsis."

"Whoever did this..."

"It was more than one." He paused for a moment. "Likely many. I'm sorry."

Jean did not say anything for a long while but a nerve twitched in his cheek. Then he said to Formento. "You will stay with us until she is healed."

Formento shook his head. "The settlement at Champ d'Asile is about to be evacuated next week. I will be returning with them to New Orleans."

"You will stay with us until she is healed. I will pay for your passage, when the time is right. And you will be richly rewarded for your services."

The doctor inclined his head.

＊

"Be quiet, Jules," Jean said. "Your sister is sleeping."

"What is wrong with Denise?"

Theodosia exchanged a glance with Jean. What would they tell him? She had been bedridden for a week.

"She is sick," Jean said. "You must not play loudly on the deck."

"Is she going to die?"

"No."

"Michel's cousin got the cholera, and he died."

"She does not have cholera."

"What does she have then?"

"Jules!" Jean's voice, which was normally soft when he spoke to his children, thundered, and Jules was so startled he cringed.

"Jules, go and play with your friend, Michel," Theodosia said quietly.

"I can't, Maman. They left. They gave up on everything. All of them. Champ d'Asile is deserted now. A big ship came and took them all away last week. All except the doctor, and he's here now. Didn't you know?"

"Oh, yes, I think I did," she said distractedly. "I forgot. Could you go down to the shop and fetch some coffee, Jules? Half a pound on our account."

"Yes, Maman." He stole a glance at his father, but he could see that it was not safe to speak to him yet. "Come along, Bandito!"

When the boy and the dog had gone, she said, "Jean, I wish..."

He looked at her and there was contempt in his glance. "Yes? You wish what?"

"I... wish there were something I could do to help."

"Oh, I think you have done enough. Your contribution has been more than sufficient."

"I never meant for her to ..."

"You told her affection was not necessary..."

"I... I only said what I believed, Jean, because you swept me away, and no affection in the world could match what I felt for you!"

"And I showed you no affection? When you cried, didn't I hold you? When you were afraid, didn't I comfort you?"

"Yes, Jean, but that... was not my affection for you. It was yours for me. I only ever felt passion! It took much longer for affection to grow in me."

"You would not know affection if it hit you in the face!"

"Do you want to hit me, Jean?"

He stopped for a moment as if considering. Then he slumped and said in a quiet, defeated tone. "No."

"Jean, will you ever forgive me?"

"There is nothing to forgive, Theodosia. You were speaking the truth. I only wish you had said it to me, and not an innocent child."

"She accused me of not loving you."

"And, apparently, she was right."

"Jean, I was only trying to explain what a flimsy thing affection is."

"Yours maybe. Not mine. Not Christina's."

"Affection is common and ordinary and hardly rare. It is something that naturally develops between a man and a woman who are married. I felt affection for Joseph. But it was not enough. It couldn't hold a candle to the passion I felt for you. That I still feel for you."

"That passion of which you speak is also a very *common* thing."

"No, it is not. It does not happen between most men and women. It is rare and beautiful."

He laughed bitterly. "Every woman I have ever taken to bed has felt it. They still do. Do you imagine I hold your pleasure cry as some peculiar mark of ... *love?*"

"You did at one time," she sobbed. "You said it proved that I loved you."

"No, I never did. You did not listen. I said it betrayed your passion and was given to keep you true. That it served the husband and not the wife. I said it was nature's way of keeping women faithful, because a man can recognize his wife's pleasure cry a long distance away, when men live like beasts in the jungle. But *I* loved *you* for something else."

"What?" she asked, breathless.

Just then Dr. Formento came up on deck. "She is asking for you, Monsieur Laffite."

⁂

"Papa, I am sorry." Denise's voice was hoarse when she started speaking, and then it broke. He offered her a glass of water from the stand beside the bed, and she painfully lifted her head off the pillow. "I betrayed you, Papa, I am so ashamed."

"You did not betray me. You have nothing to be ashamed of."

"I married Francis because I thought he was one of your men, Papa. He showed me your signature on his letter of marque."

"Denise, I didn't give him that."

"Yes, Papa. I realize that now. But I didn't know. Père Antoine also said he was working for you."

"You don't have to explain."

"He's a pirate, Papa. And I did not know until... it was too late."

He was silent for a long time. Only his hand gently caressed hers. "I don't need to know what happened. I just need you to tell me this: did Francis Neely leave you on our dock naked and bound?"

"I don't remember, Papa. I don't remember anything after he gave them leave to share..."

"Share?"

"His conjugal rights, Papa. I don't remember anything else. I'm sorry." He did not reply to this, only bowed his head and continued to hold her hand, until she said: "Papa, let go. You're hurting me."

"Denise..."

"It was after I saw what he did to the passengers, and it was an American ship. I confronted him. I knew you wouldn't allow it. But he kept telling everyone he was working for you, Papa. He let some of them go, on purpose, and only after they had witnessed the most terrible atrocities, so they could spread the story. And he said he would see you hanged for a pirate."

"He will hang first."

"He said he had orders from Gambi. But I did not know that till then."

"Francis Neely has always worked for Gambi, Denise. Everyone knows that."

"Then he gave orders that anybody who wished could share in everything that was his. And at first, I did not realize he meant me." She was not crying. Her eyes were dry, and her voice was calm. "Please, don't cry, Papa," she said reaching up to wipe something from his cheek. "If you want the marriage annulled, I have … no objection."

"No need to annul it, Denise," he said gruffly. "You will wear widow's weeds soon enough."

"If he left me on your dock like that, like what you said, naked and bound, it was my fault, Papa."

"How could it possibly be your fault?"

"Because I told him about El Cid, Papa, when we were first married. I told him what happened to the daughters of El Cid. I should not have told him that. He is not a learned man, like you, Papa, and he would not even have known about it."

He sighed. "Well, as I recall, after he killed their bad husbands, El Cid's daughters each married an honorable prince. So you have nothing to worry about."

She laughed. "You are so funny, Papa. That is like saying that Job was recompensed for his lost wife and children by getting a new wife and new children who were even better."

"Denise, are you very angry with me for

remarrying?"

"No, Papa. I know you love Emma, and I want you to be happy. But... I just don't want you to forget about me."

"I have not forgotten about you, Denise."

"But you left me there in that convent school all alone."

"I'm sorry. I did not realize you needed a husband so soon. I will find you a better husband, I promise, after I have hanged Francis Neely from the yardarms of my ship."

"No, Papa. Do not find me a husband. I don't think I like men, anymore. I would like to be a spinster from hence forward."

"A spinster?" He considered that for a moment. "Very well, you may become a spinster, if you wish. It is a good trade."

"Papa, I promise I will be good. I will not make any more trouble for you. But whatever you do, please don't send me back to the school of the Ursuline nuns."

"No. No, of course not. You will remain here with Emma and Jules and Glenn, where you belong."

"But Papa, is there room enough on this ship for me?"

"Denise, there has always been room on my ship for you." The embrace between father and daughter that followed was one that Theodosia watched discreetly and at a distance from a crack in the cabin door.

She was glad that he was a good father. She only wished he could love her as well.

Before he set out to find Francis Neely, Jean said to Theodosia: "You were right. It was not safe to leave her alone in New Orleans."

But he never said he was sorry he doubted her, and she did not know if he had forgiven her yet.

Chapter Seven
At the Hanging

Theodosia spent much of her time by Denise's bedside while Jean was away. Little Glenn played on the floor with Jules' rattle, but the older boy was seldom home, preferring to go fishing or mingling with the sailors out on the docks, Bandito always at his heels. Theodosia had long since given up on knowing Jules' whereabouts, and she trusted that the Laffite hardiness would keep him safe.

"Emma," Denise asked one day, "have you ever wondered why marriage is considered a sacred institution when at its very heart is such a vulgar act?"

Theodosia looked at her for a moment to see if this was meant as an attack against her, the usurping stepmother, but Denise seemed earnest and troubled, and so Theodosia took the question at face value. "It doesn't have to be vulgar, Denise. Not every man is a brute."

"No. That's not what I meant. I mean, why do men have to live with their wives and only go to visit their daughters once in a long while? Why couldn't it be the other way around? Why couldn't men live with their daughters, and go to visit their wives when the need arises?"

Theodosia laughed. "You do realize, Denise, that the things that happen between a husband and a wife are not limited to the bedchamber."

"I know. You can do it on the mizzen deck, too."

"No, I mean, husbands and wives speak with one

another, and they share life's struggles."

"Yes. But fathers and daughters also speak with one another and share life's struggles. So the *only* real difference is that he sleeps with the one and not with the other. And just because of that, they have built a whole institution around it! But a daughter can love her father just as much as a wife can. Why doesn't that count for anything?"

"It does count, Denise. Your father has dropped everything he was doing to pursue Francis Neely and bring him to justice. And he's sorry about leaving you alone in that convent. He told me so."

"Yes, I know I have caused a lot of trouble for Papa and for you, too, Emma. And I am truly sorry for that. But what I am asking is, why does the brothel of marriage count for more than the nunnery of daughterhood? Why do you laugh, Emma?""

"You do paint quite a picture, Denise. The brothel of marriage! How ever did you think of that? And I have never even heard the word daughterhood. I think you have just invented it!"

"Well, there's motherhood. Why isn't there daughterhood? And as for the brothel of marriage, it was Père Antoine who made me think of it, when he told me that the reason Papa took you and not me was because there was no brothel on Snake Island."

"Yes, I remember your telling me that. And as for your question, I don't know, Denise. I have sometimes wondered about that, too. I would rather not think that this is all I do for Jean and that is why he keeps me close. I would rather be a person he trusts."

"Did you know that every time Papa came to see me in New Orleans, when we dined out, the next day people were saying that Jean Laffite had been seen with his young mistress, a quadroon barely out of girlhood?"

"That was you?!"

"Well, of course, you don't think he has a quadroon mistress, do you? And I ask you, do I look like a quadroon? What is wrong with people? If somebody has dark hair and eyes, Americans immediately decide they are of African stock? The only white people are blonds with fair skin? And if they see a man dining out with a woman twenty years his junior, why do they assume it is his mistress? Would it not make more sense for it to be his daughter?"

Theodosia sighed. "People have dirty minds. They thought the same of me and my father, only in our case everyone *knew* I was his daughter. But just because he loved me more than his mistresses and spent more time with me than with them, they thought it was improper. They assumed something very foul was taking place."

"I have never heard you speak of your father before."

"My father was a very great man, and he treated me with the utmost of respect. After my mother died, he never remarried, and he made me the lady of the house. I always sat on the opposite end of the table from him when we had guests. I never lacked for anything, and he held me in high regard, and he lived with me, and only went to visit the women in his life. And for that they called him a monster."

"I wish Papa respected me like that, Emma. I was practically forced to marry somebody so that I could come here. Because he has a rule against unmarried women."

"I think that he will change that rule, Denise. And he does respect you. He is a good father."

"Papa has always been very decent, but has kept me at a distance."

"Yes."

"Decency required him not to speak to me of any of

this, and I am confused. And I don't have a mother to ask."

"I didn't have a mother, either," Theodosia said. "She died when I was twelve. My father, however, was very honest. There was nothing he could not discuss with me, even the relations between men and women. And that's why people think he was *not* decent. Well, he may not have been decent. But he was honest, and to me that means *more.* They ruined him because of me. He was forced to fight a duel for my honor. And that put an end to his career. He was a great hero, you know, in the revolutionary war. But people in power turned against him."

Denise looked over at Theodosia with a new-found respect. "Then you are also a daughter of El Cid!"

⚜

When Jean returned a month later, he brought with him a bolt of fine black cloth and presented it to Denise who was standing on the forward deck, fully recovered.

"It is for you, my pet."

"What is it, Papa?"

"It is cloth for your mourning dress. Your Aunt Yvonne will make a fine outfit for you to wear."

"Is he dead then, Papa?"

"It's official. I presented the body to the coroner myself, and we have the death certificate to prove it. You are free."

"Did you hang him, Papa?"

"Yes, Denise. Eventually, that is. After I had done several other things that we need not mention. He will harm no one ever again. And I will have a wheel made for you soon."

122

"What wheel?"

"A spinning wheel."

She smiled impishly. "Thank you, Papa. You think of everything."

⁂

"And I will cut off your balls and hang your naked, rotting corpse from the highest tree!"

Theodosia turned around from hanging laundry only to see Jules and Glenn fencing on the forward deck with two makeshift sticks, the older boy advancing menacingly toward the toddler. "Jules, what are you doing!?!"

"Nothing, Maman."

"What did you just say to your brother?"

"I wasn't saying that to Glenn, Maman, don't worry!"

"Well, who were you saying it to?"

"We were pretending, Maman."

"Really? What were you pretending?"

"I was pretending that I was Papa, and Glenn was pretending that he was Francis Neely. Isn't that right, Glenn?"

Glenn nodded with a big smile on his face.

"Jules, Glenn is only two years old. I don't think he knows what you mean."

"Yes, Maman."

"Have you finished your chart making lesson?"

"No, Maman."

"Then go work on that. Your father expects it done by this evening."

"Yes, Maman." He dropped the stick and prepared to go down below to work on his lessons. But in the doorway he turned around and asked: "What is rape, Maman?"

She hesitated. "It is a very bad thing for a man to do to a woman," she finally said. "It is taking by force what any gentleman would only take after asking permission and being granted leave."

Jules looked mystified, but he could see that he would get no more out of her, so he asked nothing else.

✤

Denise was dressed all in black with a veil that hid her face when Jean brought Francis Little by to take measurements.

"My daughter wishes to become a spinster, and so I would like you to make a spinning wheel for her."

Theodosia cringed. "Jean, I don't think she meant..."

Little smiled and asked: "Will she be needing a loom, too?"

Jean nodded. "Yes. A loom would be good. I had not thought of that. Do you know how to make a loom, Frank?"

The younger man nodded. "I can make anything out of wood."

"I will see that you have the best of materials at your disposal."

Denise did not say a thing. She hardly even moved, while this discussion ensued. She was like a black statue.

"Since we are not doing well with our farming endeavors, and we lost the colony at Champ d'Asile, I think textiles would be a good industry to invest in," Jean said. "It is something we could export, should there be a surplus. And in any event, it will avoid that ridiculous tariff they are now using to protect the larger manufacturers in the east."

"Is that really a concern, Sir? I mean, since the income at Campêche is based almost entirely on privateering?"

Jean smiled. "It is. But once Spain and Britain have been smashed to pieces and there are no more enemies to prey on, we would do well to have another industry to fall back on. Even the Karankawa do not live on fishing and hunting alone."

"Yes, they also eat people."

The blond young man's remark elicited a giggle from the veiled figure in the corner.

"That is not what I meant, Frank," Jean said, smiling. "They have been known to trade."

"What do they trade?"

"Alligator skins for cooking utensils."

The presence of Denise on board the *General Victoria* had a chastening effect on relations between Jean and Theodosia. He was not angry with her, anymore, Theodosia sensed that. But he behaved differently, almost circumspectly, as if fearing to touch her, lest the effect of the contact somehow should taint his daughter, who was watching.

Before, with each of them living oceans apart, Jean had been able to separate the two women in his life, and to allow each to shine in her own sphere. Now they were all three thrown together for many an hour, and he could not show favoritism toward one without alienating the other. Often subtle and not so subtle traps and snares were set for him by the two rivals for his affection, and Theodosia, when she was not feeling blinded by jealousy, could not help but admire the verbal *leger-de-main* with which he avoided each pitfall.

"Papa, does it bother you very much that I am here?"

"No, Denise. I am glad you are."

"But you wanted me kept away."

"I wanted to keep you safe. I swore to the memory of your mother that I would keep you safe from harm. It was the only reason I kept you away."

She paused for a moment. Then she said: "But now that you are married to Emma, you can no longer love Maman."

"No, I still love her, no less today than on the day you were born."

With a sharp glance toward Theodosia and an almost stealthy look back at her father, Denise rapid-fired the logical question that this reponse elicited: "Then if Maman had not died, you would *never* have married Emma?"

Jean looked at Theodosia, and she looked back at him with a blank expression, as if to say: Let's see how you get out of that one!

He smiled, rising to the challenge. "No, I would still have married Emma."

"But Papa, that is bigamy!"

He spread his hands. "We are not Romans, Denise."

Oddly enough, the girl accepted this. It was Theodosia who had trouble swallowing the idea. It rankled.

"Do you really think that would have worked, Jean? Me and Christina and you?"

"We shall never know," he replied. "But as I recall, you once thought I was married and loved me no less."

It was true. In the first days of their coupling she had no idea whether he was married or not. While she was relieved to find out that he wasn't, her passion for him would not have diminished if he were.

When Denise retired for the night, Jean gestured with his eyes toward Theodosia. She got up and followed him

126

silently on deck.

"Walk with me," he said and took her hand and led her onto the dock and past the *Ciel Bleu* and into the *Saragossa*. He then unlocked the strongroom and gestured for her to enter, locking the door behind him.

"Are we going to count the money?" she asked in a whisper.

He slipped his hand into her gown, and she gasped. "We can be alone here, and no one will hear us."

"I've never known you to be afraid of making noise," Theodosia laughed, aroused and eager, but not ready to let it go.

"It is not the noise *I* make that I am concerned about," he said grandly, while forcing his way into a tender spot. "It is the sounds *you* will make very soon."

She could not think clearly through the fog of her desire, but her voice, low and tremulous, rasped: "You used to laugh at my shame when every member of the crew witnessed my undoing."

"She is my daughter," he said. "I can't force her to listen to that. I can't do that to her."

"But you let me make a fool of myself in front of my sons every time before she came to join us."

"That is different. They are just little boys They don't understand."

She wished she could slap him for that, it made her so angry, but by now he had pinned her hands behind her back. Helpless as usual, she soon lost all self-control, and submitted mindlessly until the pleasure grew unbearable. The doors of the strongroom muffled her cry, and yet she imagined the sailors outside still might hear.

❊

When Edward Livingston came for another visit, the talk was again about the markets, and how the recent financial upheaval had resulted in new laws.

"Take manufacturing, for instance," he said at dinner aboard the *General Victoria*. "Before the war, we had no manufacturing as such. The weaving of cloth was largely done at home for home consumption. Every housewife knew how to spin and to weave."

"Denise is very good at it," Jean interjected.

"Thank you, Papa."

Livingston regarded the young girl, dressed all in black, but no longer veiled. "You are to be commended on your work." Then he turned back to Jean. "But... those factory-made textiles which we formerly bought from Britain prior to the war had to be supplied by local businesses as soon as we could no longer legally trade with the British."

"Well, Ed, just because it was not legal does not mean it was not done. I smuggled in many a bolt of fine cloth and sold them at auction by the yard."

"Yes, indeed," Livingston smiled. "I remember the good old days at Barataria. Nevertheless, despite the competition that smugglers offered them, local businessmen organized factories to replace the lost imports. And leading merchants, who had formerly employed their capital in foreign trade, turned to investing in the local manufacturing firms, which were now incorporated and run like banks."

"What do you mean, run like banks?" Theodosia asked.

"They are not sole proprietorships or partnerships like most businesses. They are owned by stockholders who have invested in them without in fact knowing anything about the business or being involved in its day to day operation. They are at risk only for their investment, and hence they take no interest in management."

"So who runs the businesses?"

"Charlatans, in most cases, I am afraid. And they refuse to shut down when there is no profit. From 1812 to 1815, the number of factories for the making of cloth from cotton and wool that were opened each year in the eastern states averaged sixty-five. Per year! And this is a problem now."

Jean spread out his hands. "Why is it a problem?"

"Because we are doing business with Britain again. Cotton prices have gone down. Textiles prices have gone down. Well, they didn't at once. Right after the war, prices were still going up, and the banks encouraged expansion. They even opened a stock exchange on Wall Street in New York City. The banks lent money when they ought to have reined people in. But the bubble burst, and now things are bad. People borrowed money to build these businesses and now they cannot repay their loans. And unlike home-based businesses which can simply stop spinning and weaving when there is less demand, they have employees and machinery and expenses that are not easily got rid of when the need for them no longer exists."

"But surely if they cannot pay their laborers, then the labor must cease," Jean said, in a reasonable tone of voice.

"Their laborers do not think so, and neither does management. And the stockholders are all lobbying in their favor in Washington City. So that's where the tariff comes in! It is not so much a tax to raise revenue for the government, as a means to beat the competition from abroad."

"They mean to force the American people to buy at a

higher price what can be got cheap? But did they not fight their revolution to keep just such a thing from happening?"

Livingston laughed. "Nobody remembers why we fought the revolution."

"And they call *us* pirates!"

"Jean, speaking of that, I think you handled the Neely matter a little too cavalierly. They are saying you are a pirate, because you unceremoniously hang people."

"Well, they hang people, too, and for no reason whatever. Take what they did to John Whitman."

"You mean, Andrew Whiteman."

"It does not matter what name he goes by. He's dead all the same. They hanged him. And what did he do wrong?"

Livingston laughed bitterly. "It's not whether the person you hang deserves it or not that determines that you are a pirate. It's whether he had a trial. Jury of his peers and all that."

"Well, fine. I have set up that apparatus here, for all the good it will do any man I catch thieving or molesting women. We have thirteen on each jury, so we do one better than the English. And we have panels of three judges."

"That's all well and good. But did you try Neely?"

"No. What he did was not something that can be discussed in public. And I killed him in a duel, so it was all clean. I only hanged the body after, as a sign to his men."

"I don't approve of dueling, anymore," Livingston said. "There has got to be a better way to settle disputes."

"Nothing was in dispute, Ed. It was about honor, and honor cries out for revenge."

Denise could not contain her natural exuberance for

long, though Theodosia suspected that the injury that had been done to her spirit might still be buried deep within. The girl was soon on the foredeck, dressed all in black but with her sleeves rolled up, tilting with Jules, both of them using sticks for swords. Theodosia, watching them from a distance, admired the sight, and she had to admit she was relieved that Jules had Denise for a sparring partner, rather than Glenn.

When Frank Little came by to deliver the spinning wheel, he stopped for a moment to watch the two.

"Miss Laffite," he finally said. "Where shall I set down your spinning wheel?"

She turned around, flushed and confused for a moment, and then answered: "Right here will be fine, Mr. Little."

Denise watched him as he brought the disassembled spinning wheel on board and set it up, and she watched him as he left, and Theodosia watched her watching. Then Jules and Denise began fencing again.

A week later, Jules had a new toy. Less expensive than the silver rattle, the wooden sword looked quite impressive.

"Where did you get that, Jules?" Theodosia asked.

"Frank Little made it for me. He made one for Denise, too."

She looked to Denise for confirmation. But the girl dressed all in black was concentrating on her spinning. And her wooden sword was nowhere in sight.

Once again there was to be a hanging. And though many a man had been hanged on the yardarms of a docked

131

ship, this time Jean decided to erect a gallows. He wanted to show the world that his commune was like all the civilized nations of the earth and that criminals were properly tried and executed. Naturally, he designed the gallows himself, sketching it roughly, but then he called in Frank Little to help him erect the structure, and he and Little spent some time revising the design until both were agreed it would make a very fine gallows, better than the one in front of the Cabildo.

They would try the culprits after breakfast, and the hanging would take place at noon. Jean was nothing if not punctual, once he had made up his mind about something. He did not waste time. "Attendance at the trial," he announced that morning at the breakfast table, "is optional. But I expect all of you to attend the hanging. We must present a united front and show that our values are no different from those of any other civilized people."

"Hanging is so cruel," Denise said unexpectedly. She was usually the first to exalt in a gory story. Was she thinking about Francis Neely? Theodosia wondered. But they never spoke of that, anymore.

"Cruel, perhaps," said Jean. "But not unusual. Once they see what a fine gallows I have built, those people in New Orleans will no longer think I am a pirate."

"Jean, I don't think it works that way," Theodosia said, but as usual he ignored her doubts.

"We are going to hold a public trial, and we will transcribe everything that is done, so there will be a written record of the proceedings. There will be counsel for the defendant and counsel for the state, and they will make frivolous objections to the testimony of the witnesses, which the judges will be able to sustain or overrule just as they please, based on the finest and most delicate points of law."

Theodosia laughed. "Is that what you think about trials, Jean?"

"I have seen enough of them to know how it goes. We will allow all that to take place, but it will be a speedy trial nonetheless and by noon the accused will be hung by the neck until dead and justice will be served."

"How can you know that the accused will be executed?" Theodosia insisted. "If it's a fair trial, you can't know that in advance."

"Of course, I can."

"Sentence first, verdict later, is that it?" she asked.

"But he's guilty as sin! It wouldn't be a fair trial if he weren't sentenced to hang! Come to the trial and you will see."

"Well, if it's a foregone conclusion, then I think I will sit this one out," she said. "I like my trials with an element of surprise in them. But how can you know for sure, Jean?"

"I am an expert witness for the prosecution," he replied. And he got up and walked away, leaving her quite speechless. She got up from the table and followed him up on deck. "Jean, you do know that a man is innocent until proven guilty, don't you?"

But he did not reply. She watched him go down the gang plank, and then he stopped on the dock and turned and called out: "I'm sorry, my love, I can't stop to philosophize with you, as I am off to court!" The Maison Rouge had been partially rebuilt by now, and it was there that the trial was to be held.

She laughed. Thinking about Jean's expertise, she could not help laughing. Jean, an expert witness! What was his area of expertise? Could it be alchemy?

⚜

"George Brown is in point of fact an Italian by the name of Ratti," Jean explained a couple of hours later, once the verdict had been handed in and the sentence passed. "Brown is only an alias he adopted once he made his base in New Orleans. Originally, he worked for Vincenzo Gambi. I knew him for a crook and bully, and when he applied to me for a letter of marque, I would not grant it, but someone here must have given him a commission from me in my absence, after the storm, when I was away. That means I am responsible for what he did, and it is my duty to see to it that he is hanged for a pirate and that the victims of his act of piracy are properly compensated. When the nations of the world see how swift our justice is, they will be astounded!"

"What did he do?" Theodosia asked. She noticed, from the corner of her eye, that Denise was looking very pale.

"On the night of September 27 he led a dozen men with blackened faces into the house of James Lyons in lower St. Landry Parish. He had taken two armed boats up the Mermenteau River and from there into Bayou Queue de Tortue to the Lyons home. They broke in, bound and gagged Lyons and his wife and children, and pretending to be customs inspectors, they took away everything of value in the house, including ten African slaves."

"Customs inspectors?" Theodosia asked. "Why would they say they were customs inspectors?"

Jean laughed. "Because it sounded plausible. Only robbers or customs inspectors would behave in that manner!"

"Surely not! Not American customs inspectors!"

"Theodosia, when was the last time you dealt with

customs? If something has been bought and paid for and no bribe has been given to the customs inspector, he will confiscate whatever it is. And since trading in newly arrived African slaves has been declared illegal, the men of the Revenue Service do in fact confiscate any newly arrived slaves that they find, sell them at auction to the highest bidder, and pocket the majority of the profit for themselves. French speaking people of every color, Creoles and Cajuns, are sorely afraid of the customs inspectors, so much so that a fine, brisk trade has been done by various crooks just by pretending to be customs inspectors and confiscating people's household goods."

"But, Jean, do customs inspectors really blacken their faces and tie up their victims?"

"Well, no. They generally don't. They commit robbery in open daylight under cover of legalities. But our good friend George Brown was never the sharpest, and nothing he does is subtle. So naturally the Lyons family knew at once his men were not customs inspectors. They sent word of what had happened. I have done business with them before, and they know me to be an honest and upright man. When George Brown arrived here with his stolen goods, wanting to cash them in for prize money, I knew at once what was afoot. He claimed he had gotten them off a Spanish vessel."

"But didn't you need testimony to convict him?"

"We had ten witnesses. And I appeared as an expert."

"Jean, but you were not there! You did not see the acts committed! Was the Lyons family present at the trial?"

"No, my love, they would not have been able to get here so fast. But I relayed the story of what happened, as told me by their letter."

"Your testimony ought well to have been struck down as hearsay!"

He laughed. "I should have appointed you counsel for the defendant, my dear. Your knowledge of the law is astounding!"

"And didn't the attorney you actually *did* appoint for George Brown make this objection?"

"He did indeed. He moved that the case be dismissed for want of evidence."

"And then what happened?"

"They thought we had no witnesses to the act. They had forgotten that the merchandise could speak! We introduced ten witnesses: the stolen Africans!"

"But did they speak Spanish or English or French?"

"No, my dear, they spoke a West African creole, which as it happens, I am priveleged to understand. I learned that tongue when yet a boy in Saint Domingue."

"You served as interpreter?"

"I did. And I was also sworn in as an expert witness. Did you know that expert testimony is an exception to the hearsay rule?"

She laughed: "Yes, Jean, but it's a limited exception. You can't just repeat gossip on the stand."

"I merely summarized what the Africans told me."

"Did they object very much to being stolen from their owners, Papa?" Denise asked suddenly. She had been silent and brooding all this while.

"They did indeed, Denise. The Lyons family has shown them great kindness, but Ratti and his band of robbers were very cruel and even injured one of their women. They want very much to be returned to their masters. And I am throwing in an extra slave into the bargain, to make up for the one who was injured and will not be able to work for some time."

"How considerate of you," Theodosia said, her

disapproval dripping from her tone.

"There will be another time to discuss the slavery question, Theodosia. At the moment, we have a hanging to attend. Denise, I want you to wear a colorful frock. There is no need for you to mourn any longer."

"I don't want to go," Denise said.

They turned to look at her. She was white as a sheet.

"I'm afraid that I must insist. We are to present a united front. I want my whole family at the execution. It is a matter of respectability and proper procedure. I do not want it said that I murdered Ratti and his men."

"You have his men, too?" Theodosia asked, trying to ignore Denise's knit brows and trembling lips.

"Only three of them."

"So there will be four hangings?"

"We shall see. It may not be prudent to execute all four, though all have been convicted and sentenced to death."

Dressing for a public hanging was apparently a very involved process. Theodosia lingered by Jean as he was shaving in his shirtsleeves, even though it was not yet midday, and he had shaved earlier that morning. Then he ran a comb through his side-whiskers and mustache.

"Jean..." she started to say, and he turned around to look at her.

"Are you going to wear your hair like that?"

"Like what?" she asked, annoyed.

"Put it up," he said. "Everyone will be looking at you. You must look your best."

"Everyone will be looking at *me*?" She was astounded.

"It's a hanging, Jean. They will be looking at George Brown."

"You would be surprised at how many people avert their glance at the last moment and look at something else. You must not be seen to flinch. It reflects on me and on my government."

"How?!"

"I want everyone who is here to see that we operate by rule of law and that all the proper forms of civilized behavior are observed."

"Jean, I will go, though I may not be able to help flinching. I will stand by your side and grant legitimacy to your rule, if that is what you want of me. But leave the children out of it."

"Why?"

"Denise is still recovering..."

"No. She is fine. And it's for her own sake that I am doing this."

"Jules and Glenn are too young."

"Glenn is too young," Jean said, fixing his collar. "Jules is not too young."

Theodosia put up her hair and went to check on Denise. "Are you all right?"

"Yes." But her face seemed frozen.

"Denise, you are so pale! Why are you afraid?"

"He was one of them," she whispered.

⁂

The gibbet was erected on a point overlooking the pass where all incoming vessels would see it. The body was to hang there long after life had been extinguished as a warning to others. The scaffolding below allowed for a swift and effective execution, with a sack of sand as counterbalance. Before the condemned was brought out, the mechanism was demonstrated to the delight of the crowds.

Across from the gallows was a gallery for spectators, and special makeshift balcony for the Laffites and their associates. Though the structures were new and the wood untreated, there was something distinguished in their design that recalled the finest courts of Europe.

"Papa, why must the man hang?" Jules asked. Of the four of them, he seemed the most eager for the execution.

"For the thief and pirate and brute that he is and for stealing from other people."

"But don't you do that, Papa?"

"Do what?"

"Steal from people."

"No. Never. I never steal from *people*. I only plunder the vessels of Britain and Spain."

"But is it all right to steal from Britain and Spain, Papa?"

"Yes. Because they are evil."

The boy nodded, as if that explained everything. "Are you going to hang him yourself, Papa?"

"No. Not this time, Jules. I am neither the judge nor the jury nor the executioner. He has had a proper trial, and he will have a proper execution. You see that man in the black mask?"

"Yes, Papa. But why does he wear a mask?"

"It is proper procedure. He is the executioner. Executioners always wear masks."

"But why?"

"So that no one will recognize them and seek revenge."

"It kind of looks like Uncle Reyné," Jules said. "But I thought you asked Frank Little to do this job."

"No, Jules. Frank is a carpenter. He was to build the structure." He gave a brief nod to Little who was standing behind the women. "And he did a fine job of it. Now you must be quiet, son, for they are beginning."

Theodosia was lulled for a moment into a sort of familiar trance, listening to the conversation between father and son. Training her eyes on the man being led to the platform, she was able to make out his fear in his odd, forced gait, but she quashed any last bit of empathy that she might have felt. Then when the noose was forced round his neck, she heard a muffled cry behind her and turned around to see Denise swoon. Frank Little caught her just in time.

The girl came to at once, and Little steadied her till she found her balance and looked up at him, confused. Nodding curtly and stepping back, all he said was: "Miss Laffite."

By the time Theodosia turned her gaze back toward the gibbet, George Brown was hanging by the neck, broken and lifeless, his feet dangling in the air. The crowds were roaring.

"What are they saying, Papa?" Jules asked, as it was hard to make out the disjointed cries.

"They want clemency for the other three men convicted. So I will not have them hanged. I will put them in a rudderless boat adrift in the ocean with no provisions and leave them to repent of their crimes."

Chapter Eight
The Beginning of the End

The next morning, there was a dense fog extending over the water. Jules, who had climbed the mainmast to get a better view of the hanged man on the pass and because he hoped to catch a glimpse of the doomed men set adrift, was the first to spot the intruder. "There's a ship out there, Papa!"

The masts of the unidentified vessel could be seen out beyond the sandbar, despite the fog, though not much else of the ship was visible.

"It is an American cruiser," Jean declared, looking through his spyglass. "And as they have not made their business here known, I must assume that they are planning to make war on us."

"Surely not, Jean!" Theodosia exclaimed.

"Fetch me some paper and I will send them a letter of warning," he said. "I want to give them every opportunity to make their business here known."

The letter he wrote surprised Theodosia, not so much by its manner, but by certain details in the wording

To the Commandant of the American cruiser off the port of Galvez Town

Sir—

I am convinced that you are a cruiser of the Navy ordered by your government. I have therefore deemed it proper to inquire into the cause of your lying before this port without communicating your intention. I shall by this message inform you that the Port of Galvezton belongs to and is in the possession of the Republic of Texas, and was made a port of entry the 9th of Oct. last. ____And whereas the supreme congress of said republic have thought proper to appoint me as governor of this place, in consequence of which, if you have any demands on said government, you will please to send an officer with such demands ____Whom you may be assured will be treated with the greatest politeness and receive every satisfaction required. But if you are ordered, or should attempt to enter this port in a hostile manner, my oath and duty to the government compels me to rebut your intentions at the expense of my life.

To prove to you my intentions toward the welfare and harmony of your government, I send enclosed the declarations of several prisoners, who were taken in custody yesterday, and by a court of enquiry appointed for the purpose, were found to be guilty of robbing the inhabitants of the United States of a number of slaves and other property.

The gentlemen bearing this message will give you any other reasonable information relating to this place that may be required.

Jn Laffite

"The Republic of Texas?" Theodosia asked when once she had read the letter. "Since when? I thought you were representing the Republic of Mexico or the Mexican Congress or Cartagena. Since when has there been a Republic of Texas, and under whom do you serve as Governor?"

"Since it became expedient," he replied blandly. He then sent for two men to row up to the American schooner and present his missive to its captain.

The response came together with a certain Lt. James McIntosh, who saluted smartly before delivering his captain's reply.

To the commander of the forces at Galvezton

U.S. Schooner Lynx
Off Galvezton, Nov. 8, 1819

Sir— Your note of yesterday has been received, stating the execution of William Brown, the chief of the boats, and you having sent in pursuit of John Hale, William Thompson and Charles Slater, who have been previously sent from Galvezton. From the disposition evinced by you to bring to justice all those who have committed direct acts of piracy on the citizens of the United States, I am induced to believe that should they, or John Kelly, John Lightner and George Kerth, who appear to be the only survivors not at present in custody, come at any future period in your power, that they will be detained in confinement until they

can be sent to the United States for trial. I
have returned to you the passage boat belonging
to you which was taken by my boats on the
fifth inst. You will excuse me for not accepting
your kind and polite invitation to visit
Galvezton. The weather will not permit my
leaving the vessel at sea, but any communication
delivered to the officer who has charge of this
will be duly received.

I am, Sir, yours etc.

J.R. Madison, commanding US schr. Lynx

Jean invited McIntosh to a tour of Galvez Town and
in a very calm and friendly tone explained to him the nature
of his sovereignty and the legitimacy of the trial that was
already held.

"My commader has instructed me to arrest all those
still alive of the band of robbers so that they may undergo a
proper trial in a court of law in the United States," Lt.
McIntosh explained.

"But the men whom I sent adrift without provisions
have already undergone a proper trial," Jean replied.

"No, I mean a real trial," McIntosh interrupted. "With
due process and all that."

"They have had due process," Jean insisted. "And a
speedy trial. Does not your constitution provide for that?
And yet people languish in the Cabildo for months and
years, only to be hanged for crimes they never committed.
My justice, in contrast, is swift and unerring!"

"But to send men out adrift at sea without provisions
is barbaric!" McIntosh remonstrated.

"They were sentenced to hang. But my people are
very kind hearted, and they demanded clemency. They did

not mind seeing the ringleader hang, but they would not have stood for four hangings in a row. And since I have not much of a prison, I thought it would be fitting to send them out among the beasts."

By the time Lt. McIntosh's visit had ended, Jean had quite won him over. The three men who had been sent out adrift were recaptured and presented as prisoners to the Americans. The stolen slaves and one extra were returned to their owners along with all the stolen goods recovered, and all was right with world. Jean even gave each slave an extra outfit of brand new well-tailored clothes to make up for what they had been through. Theodosia noticed how happy the women were with their new dresses. The *Lynx* sailed away, and the "Republic of Texas" remained intact.

"So tell me, Jean," Theodosia asked again. "Where did you get this idea of a Republic of Texas?"

"I will tell you, my dear, if you have time for a rather long story. It happened like this. As you know, the United States gave up all claims to the territory west of the Sabine River when your good friend John Quincy Adams signed that treaty with Ambassador Onis of Spain."

"He is not *my* good friend!"

"In any event, everything that he sent George Graham to tell me at the time of his visit here was false, and even if it had been true, it no longer could be. And, yet...!"

"And yet?" she asked.

"Those rascals, Graham, Ripley, Ross, Patterson, and Oliver have been financing thieves like Adair, Long, Johnson, Smith and Bigelow. They were stealing merchandise off my boats with the blessing of those politicians. As just one example of this practice, let me tell you about what happened to Ortiz."

"Ortiz?"

"Hernon Ortiz is one of my captains. I sent him this spring with a cargo for Mr. Manuel Lisa and Mr. Hempstead in St. Louis. The ship was captured near Natchez. All the merchandise on board and the band of slaves were taken, as was the captain, Ortiz."

"How awful! When did this happen, Jean?"

"Around April 10 of this year, or thereabouts. Captain Ortiz returned to Galvez Town in June. He was very oddly dressed, in a fur cap and a fur coat."

"In June? Here in Galvezton? Wasn't it too hot for fur?"

"Yes, at first I thought he had gone mad. But he told me about his capture, and he gave news of my enemies. Although Ortiz could not speak English well, he understood what some of his captors were saying. He told me that they addressed each other by the titles of General Adair and General Long. He heard them speak ill of the Bowie brothers, because they, too, had designs on Texas and were members of my commune. At first I did not give much credence to the warning from Ortiz, and I reassigned him to Venezuela, where Uncle Reyné could keep an eye on him."

"But...?"

"In May, James Long proclaimed himself the president of the Republic of Texas. He had backing from James Wilkinson. In fact, his wife is Wilkinson's niece."

"How do you know this?"

"Common knowledge."

"It is not common knowledge to me."

"You forget that I served as a spy under James Wilkinson for many years. Anyway, Long has the backing of both the American Navy under Patterson and the clandestine Spanish plotters under Wilkinson. So rather than stand up to him directly, when he offered me the

146

opportunity to serve as the Governor of Galvezton under his new government, I demurred."

"You demurred?"

"I didn't say no. That way he could take me for an ally. When the *Lynx* came to call, I judged it best to conjure up Long's authority, rather than my own. I think I gambled well. Since Patterson is known to be backing Long, the Navy and the Revenue Service are bound to hold his Republic of Texas in high regard at the moment."

⁂

Denise was at her spinning wheel, when Jules came in to show her what he got.

"Look, Denise! It's a miniature gallows, with gibbet and rope and all."

She stopped to look, then wrinkled her nose. "Where did you get that?"

"Mr. Little gave it to me."

"Why?"

"He said he thought I might like to have it as a memento of the hanging. Seeing as it's almost Christmas and all."

"Which hanging? There have been so many lately."

"The first one since the gallows were erected. The hanging of George Brown."

"Well, that's nice. You can add it to your collection."

Jules only had three toys. The silver rattle, the wooden sword and now the miniature gallows.

"He made something for Glenn, too, but Maman is away with him at the shops, so I can't give it to him yet. See?"

It was a little spinning top, whittled out of plain wood

and left unpainted.

"Well, I hope he does not swallow it. He still puts everything in his mouth."

"And he gave me something for you, too."

"He did?"

"Well, don't you want to see it?"

"Sure."

The boy produced from his pocket a curious wooden trinket. "It's a necklace!"

"It looks more like a chain," she said.

Each link was laced through another link, and there was no way to undo it. There were no cracks or gaps where any link in the chain could be taken apart and separated from the others.

"How did he make it?" she asked, examining carefully to see what the magic was.

"He said he whittled it all from a single piece of wood. He said a chain is only as strong as the weakest link. Well, aren't you going to wear it?"

"Why would I want to wear a wooden chain round my neck? I could get splinters."

"Suit yourself." And Jules went back up on deck.

But when the boy had gone, she tried it on. It fit perfectly.

※

Edward Livingston came to call again at the end December of 1819 for a legal conference with Pierre and Jean. He brought with him the latest news from New Orleans. "Vincenzo Gambi is dead!"

"Did Daniel Patterson finally get him?" Jean asked. "He seemed incredibly incompetent whenever it came to real

148

pirates."

"Well, in a manner of speaking, he did capture him, but the man was already dead. So perhaps the only real pirates the U.S. Navy can handle are dead pirates."

"Who killed him?"

"His crewmen. Using his own axe. They cut off his head when he was asleep."

"Cut off his head!" Jules exclaimed.

"Yes, I know your interest in decapitations, Jules," Livingston said, smiling. "I thought you would enjoy this story."

"What happened?" Jules asked eagerly, while Theodosia grimaced at Livingston.

"Well, apparently he had short-changed the men by two thousand dollars in divying up their latest prize money. So while he was taking a nap on deck, his head resting on a spar, one of the men picked up his bloody axe which he often used on victims and chopped his head off!"

"No! Is that really true, Uncle Edward?"

"Well, I read it in the *Louisiana Courier*, and the papers would never lie." Livingston winked. "Especially not about something this interesting."

"Hmmm," Jean intoned.

"For instance, the papers say that you have joined up with General Long, Jean, in his new venture, the Republic of Texas."

"Do they?"

"They published your correspondence with Lt. Madison of the *Lynx*."

"Really? And who gave it to them?"

"I suspect it was leaked by McIntosh, who is trying to make a name for himself."

"That fellow was a little too jolly."

"The sad thing about Gambi's death," Pierre said laconically, "is that he still owes me $250.00."

"Haven't you collected that yet?" Jean asked.

"The wheels of justice grind exceedingly slow."

"Speaking of wheels and justice," Livingston asked, looking at Jean, "how do you plan to handle the *Le Brave* case?"

"Can't you get it dismissed?"

"No, Jean, I can't. I can, however, delay its coming to trial indefinitely."

"What good will that do?"

"Lots of legal fees for Ed," Pierre said, laughing. "That's all the American legal system is good for."

"What is the *Le Brave* case?" Theodosia asked. It was the first she had heard of it.

"Very unpleasant business," Livingston said. "They are tying a noose round all privateers' necks. I'm afraid it's the end for that line of business."

"They captured one of my ships," Jean said in answer to Theodosia's confused glance. "And it wasn't one of those rogue captains, like George Brown or Francis Neely, who really were pirates and deserved to be hanged. Jean DesFarges and Robert Johnson are good, decent men. They are not pirates, and they did not commit an act of piracy."

"Well, then what did happen?"

"They fired on an American vessel, that's what happened," Livingston said.

"But only in self-defense."

"That does not matter, Jean. The United States government maintains that you are *not* entitled to defend yourself against them. When asked to stop, you must surrender, even if you have done no wrong. It is really the same principle that was involved in the Whiteman case. He

150

shot in the direction of a customs officer and missed, and he shot only after being shot at first, but still they found him guilty."

"What possible principle would prevent a man from standing his ground when attacked?"

"The principle that self-defense is not allowed to citizens, if it is the government that attacks them."

"That can't be an American principle," Jean said. "Thomas Jefferson would never have agreed to that."

"Jean," Theodosia said, sighing softly, "Thomas Jefferson arrested my father using General Wilkinson's soldiers as police officers on American soil. They held him without bail and suspended the right of habeas corpus. He was then to be tried for treason, but they could not find any instance in which he had levied war against the United States, because, of course, he hadn't. But some of the men who followed him had resisted arrest on Blennerhassett's Island. When a United States military officer had come to arrest them, they refused to go, and when he threatened them, they even turned their guns on him. This was the act of levying war against the United States government that the Jefferson administration had meant to rely on to convict my father of treason."

"But he wasn't convicted, was he?"

"No, Jean, he wasn't, because Justice John Marshall ruled that since my father wasn't even there on Blennerhassett's Island when that happened, he could not be held responsible for their act."

"Is that true?" Jean asked Livingston.

"Yes. It's true," Livingston admitted. "No ruling was ever made to the effect that the men on Blennerhassett's Island, who were in fact minding their own business and not levying war, were entitled to resist arrest under false charges. But then again, they were never captured."

"But wasn't the whole purpose of the bill of rights to grant citizens the right to resist search and arrest without just cause?" Jean asked.

"Yes. But that presupposed that the government would not violate the bill of rights once it passed into law."

"But if they do violate it, you have the right to resist!"

"It is what we have been arguing all along," Livingston said. "But the government does not agree. They say you should surrender at once and argue the case in court."

"Right, after they have taken all your property and searched your person and uncovered all your secrets!" Pierre said. "And after you have suffered a stroke while rotting for months in their stinking jail cell!"

There was a short silence.

"But what exactly happened?" Theodosia finally asked. "I mean, with *Le Brave?*"

"I bought a new ship," Jean said, "christened it *Le Brave,* and I sent DesFarges and Johnson, with a crew of sixteen men on board to take it on its maiden voyage. They encountered a Spanish vessel, the *Filomena,* bound from Pensacola to Havana, and they engaged it and captured it as a prize. It was all perfectly legal, according to the letter of marque that I granted them. And it was a fine prize, laden with a cargo of raisins, flour, lard, beef, peas and three thousand dollars in gold and silver coin."

"And of course, seeing that the *Le Brave* had done so well, two American cutters at once attempted to intercept it and get the spoils for themselves," Pierre said.

"It was the *Alabama,* commanded by Don Gomez Taylor and the *Louisiana* under Lt. Harris Loomis," Livingston interjected.

152

"It was actually the next day, off the Florida Keys," Jean said. "DesFarges fired a musket volley at the *Louisiana*, but when the volley was returned, he surrendered."

"They are planning to make much of that musket volley," Livingston said. "It was unfortunate that he fired at all."

"Agreed," Jean said. "He should not have. But what is the case in a nutshell? That he fired on an American vessel when two of them were attacking him and requiring him to surrender? Or is it that he took the *Filomena* as prize?"

"They are going after your letter of marque, Jean," Livingston said. "They are claiming that you had no authority to grant it. They want to hang DesFarges and Johnson and their entire crew as pirates."

"If they are pirates, then I am a pirate."

"That's right, Jean," Livingston said sadly. "They're planning to hang you, too."

There was a long silence. Theodosia felt sick to her stomach.

"Is it because I am not an American that they want to destroy me?" Jean finally asked.

"No. Honestly, it's not. I think it's because you are making a profit and that you pay with silver and gold, while they are short on specie," Livingston said. "This August, Judge Richard Peters handed down a decision against one of DeForest's privateers in Philadelphia. Here, I have the clipping. Let me read you a portion."

It is a disgrace to the character of American citizens thus to prostitute themselves in acts of nefarious robbery and plunder, under the mask of assisting the Spanish patriots of South America, as those are termed whose cause many of our deluded or vitiated citizens seek to

*espouse; when in fact they are pursuing selfish
and sordid objects for their private emolument.*

"In short, they object to our making a profit!" Pierre exclaimed.

"Yes. The prosecution of the *Le Brave* case is planning to make much of your contract that sets forth how many shares each member of the crew receives, as if this somehow proves your motives were base. They will not object to privateering so much as profiteering."

"But if you take the profit out of privateering," Jean said, "then there will be nothing to fund private armies with. Then they will be stuck with a standing army and a standing navy, and their own citizens will pay for it all with the taxes on their daily bread."

"Yes," Livingston sighed. "It's the British model. Under early British law, piracy once was called petty treason. Why treason? Why not robbery? Because plundering ships was the King's prerogative. Taking it upon yourself was an affront to the established sovereignty of the Crown. Nothing to do with stealing. Meanwhile, this is the sort of swill they are selling to the populace." He pulled out another clipping.

Norwich CT Courier
Oct. 20, 1819
N. Orleans Sept. 15.

The U.S. revenue cutter Louisiana, Captain J. Loomis, and the Alabama, also a revenue cutter, which were lately built at New-York, arrived at the Bayou St. John yesterday, having in company the Spanish schr. Philomena, which they recaptured from a pirate on the 29th ult. off the Dry Tortugas. The pirate is also brought in. On that day they fell in with an American schooner bound from this port (New Orleans), on board of which the pirate had placed a number of Spanish gentlemen and Ladies, who had been passengers in the Philomena. From their information, Captain Loomis supposed that the pirate could not be very distant, and determined to look out for her. Eight hours afterwards, accordingly, he espied two sail, one of which stood for him, and on being required by the Captain of the Alabama to send her boat on board, fired a volley of small arms; she was soon silenced, however, and taken possession of. She proved to be a schooner called the Brave, fitted out at New-Orleans, carrying two guns and twenty-four men, and commanded by a man who calls himself Le Fage. Her prize the Philomena, was about a mile astern during the action, but was soon overhauled and re-captured. In the slight contest, which preceded the capture of the Brave, the Alabama had four of her men wounded, two of them, including the first lieut, dangerously – the pirate lost 6 men killed. The remainder of her crew, to the number of 13, were safely lodged in prison last evening. The Brave had on board a number of Spanish prisoners, who are thus happily relieved from a captivity, which most probably would have terminated, if they had not fallen in with the revenue cutter, by their being compelled to walk the plank. The pirate had a printed commission, the date of which was blank, signed Humbert, governor of Texas.

A passenger in the *Emma*, who conversed with Capt. Loomis, states that at the time the above pirate was captured, she had not been in possession of her Spanish prize long enough to commit the outrages upon the passengers which were threatened, but had stripped them of nearly all their clothes. The pirate approached with sweeps within pistol shot of the cutter before she fired – only three men in the cutter were wounded, one of them, it was feared, dangerously. The pirates were all lodged in prison at New-Orleans. The vessel had been regularly cleared out at New-Orleans for Pensacola.

We learn, by the above passenger, that the piratical establishment at Barataria from whence the recent expeditions into the Mississippi were made, had been surprised by one of the U.S. cruisers, and entirely broken up.

"They seem a little behind the times," Jean said ruefully, "if they think our establishment at Barataria has only just now been broken up."

⁕⁕

It was dark. She awoke drenched in sweat, her feet kicking at the blanket, and her mouth crying out words she never meant to say. "No! Jean!"

"What is it?" He was right there beside her, and there was nothing to fear, but she was still afraid.

She buried her head in his chest. "I'm sorry if I woke you."

155

"I wasn't asleep."

"You weren't? Well, why not? You should sleep." But her arms were hugging him too tight.

"Were you dreaming?" His voice was soft and reassuring.

"Just a bad dream. It was nothing."

"Tell me about it."

"I don't want to."

"What are you afraid of?"

"If I tell you it might come true."

"That's just superstition."

"Is it?"

"Yes. Tell me. I command it."

She laughed. He could not force her to tell him. She could always make up something else, anything but that awful nightmare. "Well... It was..."

"No. I mean the truth."

Mindreader that he was, she could never fool him. "I... It was awful, Jean. It was a hanging. They had had a trial about the Filomena, and everyone who hates us was there. Antonio de Sedella testified that you were an unrepentant sinner and would burn in the fires of hell. And Daniel Patterson said you were a bloodthirsty pirate who deflowered maidens and threw them without their undergarments into the waters of the deep."

"Without their undergarments!" He laughed.

"And Governor Claiborne was there ranting about hellish banditti. And... John Quincy Adams was there, too, in a wig looking like a British barrister. He said he was going to pass a resolution in the senate condemning everything you did, whether they convicted you or not. And on the jury there were nothing but priests and monks and bankers."

"Priests and monks and bankers!"

156

"It's not funny, Jean. And they were leading you to the gallows. And you said not to worry because you had it all under control. You said you were a god and so you never could die. So even if it looked like you were dead, you really weren't. But I knew you were lying, and you only said that to make me feel better!"

"Well, that was very considerate of me, don't you think?" he chuckled.

"No, it wasn't! I was so angry, and then they put the noose round your neck and ..."

He kissed her on the lips to silence her. Then, when she had calmed a little, he said: "I promise you, Theo, they won't hang me."

"How can you promise that?"

"They would have to catch me first, remember?"

"Miss Laffite."

Denise was dyeing some of the threads she had spun and hanging them to dry out on deck. Startled, she turned around.

"Mr. Little."

"I have asked permission from your mother to call on you." He indicated Theodosia who was watching them from a discreet distance. Glenn, sitting at her feet, was playing with his spinning top a few yards away.

"She is not my mother."

"Really? But she looks just like you. The resemblance is uncanny."

Denise sighed. "My father chose her for the resemblance."

"To you?"

"No. No... To his grandmother. They say she looks like his grandmother, and so do I. My father adored his grandmother, but I don't remember her. She died when I was two. And my mother died when I was born."

The young man was at a loss for a long moment, and he cleared his throat before he spoke again. "That is a fine color you have chosen for your thread."

"Thank you, Mr. Little." She did not look at him, and her words were only a social reflex.

"My given name is Francis," he said.

She wheeled to face him, flushed. "I could never like anyone named Francis!"

At this insane reply, he took a step back, for it looked almost as if she were about to draw a knife on him. "Oh, I... I'm sorry to hear that." He turned to go.

"I meant no disrespect, Mr. Little," she softened. "I did not mean to offend you."

He stopped and turned back. "No, of course not. I can see that you didn't."

"I know you cannot help being named that, but I could never utter such a name."

"Yes. Of course." He shuffled his feet, then looked back at her, hope returning. "It is utterly unutterable." He winced when she giggled at his verbal awkwardness, then he rallied. "I mean, it is a hard name to go by. My friends find it difficult to utter, too," he said cheerfully. "That's why they call me Frank."

"Oh." Her eyes brightened. "Oh! That is completely different! Frank is a fine name."

Theodosia, from her post as dueña halfway across the foredeck, smiled at this exchange. She had not consulted with Jean about Frank Little's suit for his daughter's hand.

158

She had decided that for once, she would make a command decision on her own. After all, Jean had his hands full with all the men who were turning on him of late.

⚹

A delegation was sent to Galveztown by the United States government to investigate the reports that the Laffites were running a nest of pirates, following the *Le Brave* incident. George Graham headed up the committee, together with Mssrs. Johnson, Oliver and Davis.

"My government is against Spain and England," Jean told them, "I will never abandon it, except under the condition that the United States will take over here and occupy the Antilles as well as Florida."

Graham chuckled. "I am more interested in loans at favorable interest rates from Spain than I am in taking over any of its territories." It was clear that he planned to send an unfavorable report to Washington.

⚹

Pierre was still in Galvez Town on New Years' Day. 1820. He delayed his return to New Orleans, because the public sentiment was so very "anti-pirate" at the moment.

"We need an exit strategy," Pierre confided to Jean one evening after the meal.

"Why would we need that?" Jean asked testily.

"It is time to move on."

"I don't think so."

"Be reasonable. Ed told you there is no way for us to win the *Le Brave* case. DesFarges and Johnson are dead men walking."

"No! No, it is our duty to save them."

"It is our duty – to our families, to our wives and children," – here he paused to look meaningfully at Theodosia and Denise – "to save our own necks. It is only a matter of time before they come after us with a fleet of revenue service cutters."

Jean was stubborn, but Pierre, as the elder brother, though not a leader of men, had considerable influence. "What did you have in mind?" Jean finally asked.

"I have taken the liberty of drafting a letter to Daniel Patterson which I plan to send on my return. Here. Take a look."

New Orleans January 3, 1820

To Commodore D. F. Patterson, commanding officer of the New Orleans Station:

Sir——

Persuaded that the communication, of which this letter is the object, can conveniently be made to you only; it will, I hope, be received as an apology for the liberty I take of addressing myself to you.

Too long since, the names of the Laffites have been the object of general execration, as well here as abroad; tarnished and devoted to contempt in publications without any foundation; and always assimilated and attached to a gang of pirates of all countries, the audacity of which increases with impunity, and who have lately committed depradations and atrocities of all kind on the sea coast, and even within the jurisdiction of this State. It would not be difficult for me to prove that such Banditti never were engaged, kept in pay or protected by me or my Brother, in our different transactions at Galvezton; and his late conduct in that country, with regard to one of them, ought to destroy the least suspicion

But, as the non-ratification of the treaty by Spain gives to the government of the United States the jurisdiction as far west as the Rio Bravo del Norte under the purchase of Louisiana; and as the establishment at Galveztown was formed as conquered from Spain, by the Mexican Republic and the Republic of Texas; to put an end to all things and to show to the whole world that I never contributed to the violation of the sacred rights of nations, or would offer resistance or offence to the Government of the United States; and in view of restoring all confidence to the foreign trade directing itself towards this place; and to destroy all fears which the establishment of Galveztown might occasion; I now offer myself to you, willingly and at my own risk and expense, to clear Galveztown, and to disband all those who are found there; taking the engagement for myself and my Brother, that it shall never serve as a place of Rendezvous for any undertakings with our consent, or our authorization. If the offer I make to you, Sir, can receive approbation, I shall stand in need of no other thing but the necessary permit to prevent any embarrassment in the enterprize, offering at the same time any satisfactory security for its unforeseen results, with permission to all those to be found there to retire where they may choose.

If my demand is accepted, nothing shall be wanted on my part to bring it to a good result; and if you contribute to the general welfare by securing the Commerce and inhabitants against the attempts of Ruffians; I shall be indebted to you, Sir, for giving me the opportunity of striking out the odious epithets affixed to my name by my enemies; and of evincing to the Government of the United States my earnest desire to comply with the Laws; and as far as may be in my power to conduce to the safety of the Commerce of this Port, and ridding the Gulf of Mexico of Cruizers obnoxious to the Government.

I remain, Sir, your most humble and obedient Servant.

Pierre Laffite

P.S. In case you take the present in consideration, I beg leave to call on you, on the day you may be pleased to appoint.

"I will send him a barrel of fine port wine," Pierre explained. "As a down payment for the exorbitant bribe he will undoubtedly require for our safe conduct out of the mouth of hell."

"The treaty with Spain hasn't been ratified yet?" Theodosia asked, reading over Jean's shoulder.

"Not yet. And once it is, the Viceroy will show no quarter," Pierre asnwered. "Do you imagine that, after cutting his ties with de Sedella, Jean will have any help from the Spaniards?"

"I'll be damned if I grovel before that traitor, Patterson," Jean said, fuming.

Pierre smiled. "That, dear brother, is why I have taken it upon myself to grovel for the both of us. It's the only way I see to get safe passage out of what is otherwise bound to be a death trap. Let me send it to him when I get back to New Orleans, and let's see what happens. If you are not satisfied with the terms, you could always repudiate my offer. You could say I never consulted you."

Theodosia thought that Jean would say no, that he would have no part in such a base capitulation. But he did not look at Pierre, only nodded gruffly. "All right."

That's when she understood how grave the situation really was. It was the beginning of the end.

Chapter Nine
The Embers of Galveztown

"Papa says that every woman secretly longs for a pleasant little house on the shore," Denise said, not looking at Frank Little, but minding the warp and woof of her loom. "But I have never wanted a house on the shore. I've only ever longed for a ship."

"Then I will build you a ship."

"Make one for me, too," Jules interjected. "Could you make one with real sails this time? I don't like wooden sails."

"I can make you the ship," Little said smiling. "But it is your sister you must ask for the sails, if you want them to be real."

"Will you, Denise? Will you make me the sails?"

"I will have to see the ship first, so I know how big to make them."

"All right. What will you want in return?" he asked.

"Ten minutes?"

"The sailors on the docks say ten minutes is long enough to make a baby," he teased. "And I promised Maman I would watch you."

"I have no intention of making a baby, Jules. I just want to converse with Mr. Little in private. "

"All right. Ten minutes. I won't tell."

When he had gone, there was suddenly a dreadful silence in the room, which she filled, in due time with a sigh.

"Denise, I... can't tell you how highly I regard you," he finally said, his voice stiff and formal.

"I am honored by your regard... but..."

"But...?"

"But there's no use."

"Why?"

"Because I don't want a house by the shore."

"How about a cottage in the woods? A castle near a lake? A chateau in the mountains?"

"A house is a house no matter what you call it. It's not a ship. You can't sail away in a house. That's what Papa says."

"But why must you sail away?"

"Because they *always* come for us in the end. If we could not sail away, we would be doomed."

Theodosia walked in just then with Glenn in tow and some goods from the shops on the quay. "Where's Jules?"

"He stepped out for a moment."

"Did I miss anything?"

Denise shrugged. "We were discussing seaworthiness."

As the two were standing at least a yard apart, Theodosia felt certain there was no danger that she had failed them as a dueña by her brief absence.

There were two ledger books on Jean's writing desk, and he was checking the figures in one against the other. Jules was asleep on his cot, Glenn was curled up in the laundry basket, and Theodosia was in her night gown and watching him hopefully. "Come to bed."

Jean rubbed his eyes. "I can't. There's a discrepancy in the figures. I have to resolve it. And it does not help that it has become so hard to focus on the ciphers."

"Maybe you need spectacles."

He looked at her ruefully. "I am *not* that old."

But he was. He was old enough to be the father of three grown children. Just not old enough to admit it yet. He was not quite forty, but it was close. Two years had passed since his meeting with John Quincy Adams in December of 1818. Over a year had gone by since the cordial visit of Lt. McIntosh. It had been only a year ago that they had sat with Edward Livingston and Pierre and discussed the *Le Brave* case and the outlook for DesForges and Johnson and the crew. The case had not yet gone to trial, but it had long ago been tried in the press. There were the stories in the papers of atrocities committed against dainty ladies stripped of their undergarments, and DesFarges and his crew were depicted as hellish banditti engaged in acts of debauchery. The fact that the *Filomena* was a Spanish vessel owned by a Spanish subject and flying the Spanish flag was conveniently forgotten, and much was made of the ownership of its cargo by American merchants. And the beautifully crafted letter of marque and contract for equitable partition of the prize money was seen as of no legal value, just honor among thieves. Already conviction was a foregone conclusion. From the beginning there had been no hope. If DesFarges was a pirate, then Jean Laffite, the owner of the vessel, must be a pirate, too. He could be sentenced to hang in absentia, and then a fleet or Revenue Service ships might be despatched to Galvez Town to carry out the sentence. But Pierre's letter to Patterson had yet to result in a meeting.

And now with the vultures circling and the rats

leaving the sinking ship, many of Jean's men, the worst of them and the basest, sensing that his days were numbered, had begun openly pilfering.

"Jean, maybe tomorrow, in daylight, you can focus better."

"No, tomorrow, I will have to confront Jean Marotte. He has been stealing from me. I'm fairly sure."

"How do you know?"

"I sent him and James Campbell out together, on November 10."

"You mean last year?"

"No. This year. I gave them two vessels, one a schooner and the other just a sloop. They were to cruise along the northern coasts of South America and Southern Mexico. They captured some slaves and other cargo and some bars of silver and gold, and they kept double ledgers, before they split the cargo into the two vessels. Jean Marotte delivered the slaves and the other goods entrusted to him. But he seems to have kept the silver and gold to himself. His ledger does not mention it at all."

He kept poring over the books until Theodosia fell asleep, and the next morning she woke to find him in bed sleeping beside her, with little Glenn between them. She did not know how many hours of sleep he could have gotten or how Glenn had moved from the basket to the bed.

Jean summoned Marotte as soon as he was up, and with the family still at breakfast the man appeared.

"Have a seat," Jean said to Marotte. "I have some questions."

Marotte pulled up a chair. "Questions?"

"I can't seem to square the two ledgers. There are some things unaccounted for in your recent delivery."

"Such as?"

"Such as all the silver and gold bars that James Campbell entrusted to you."

Jules shifted in his chair. Glenn coughed. Denise looked up from her novel.

"Oh. Yes. That."

"Can you explain?"

"Well, you see, it was a rough voyage... and... the gold and silver bars fell ... overboard."

Jean laughed. "What a calamity!" But when he stopped laughing, he asked: "Where have you hidden them?"

"You don't believe me?"

"No, I'm afraid not."

"Are you calling me a liar?"

"Yes." Jean's voice was very soft and calm.

"Well, then that ... is an affront to my honor."

Jean nodded. "I can see that it would be."

"Well, are you going to take it back?"

"I'm afraid I can't. But we can fight a duel over it, if you wish."

"Well, all right then."

"Pistols or swords?"

"I ... uh ... "

"Would you like to drink some coffee first, Monsieur Marotte?" Theodosia interjected. She had been witness to enough duels in the past few years to know the drill.

"Yes, thank you."

The coffee at Jean's table was always the blackest. Few could stomach it. Marotte was no exception. In a moment it began to work its way to his gut, and from there to his brain. "Jean, please, I'm sorry," he began to mutter, his voice shaking.

"What?" Jean asked. "I'm not sure I heard you."

"I'm sorry! Forgive me! Please, forgive me, Jean! I'm

sorry!" he cried and got up and prostrated himself at Jean's feet.

"You're sorry? About what?"

"I took the gold and the silver. I'll give it back, I promise!"

"And your honor, how can you get that back?"

"Please! Don't kill me!"

Jean slapped him hard on the face. "You will return the bars of silver and gold today, and you and your associates will leave Galvez Town by sundown, never to return!"

"Yes, Jean." Marotte slunk out, not turning his back on Jean until he was out the door.

"Do you trust him, Papa, to do as you say?" Denise asked blandly.

"I trust that he is a coward," Jean replied. "His fear will make him obey. He has always been a coward."

"Then why did you hire him, Papa?" Jules asked.

"Good men are hard to find."

⚜

"Good men are hard to find," Denise said to Theodosia, as she was hanging her newly woven cloth to dry next to the family's laundry. "Do you think that is true?"

"Yes."

"Are most men cowards, Emma?" The girl's face was earnest, as if her whole life depended on it.

"I ... don't know, Denise. I only know that very few are brave. But ... there is a world of shades of grey between craven cowards and courageous heroes. Most men fall somewhere in between."

"I could never marry a coward."

"Do you think Frank is a coward?"

"No. I... just have no evidence that he is brave."

Theodosia laughed. "I think he is very brave to risk your father's wrath."

"But he hasn't even touched me, Emma."

"It took courage to talk to you at all. And he did touch you. Remember? When you fainted at the hanging? It was he who caught you and helped you to your feet."

"Yes. He is very kind. But kindness is no substitute for courage."

"No. It's not."

⚓

"I heard back from Patterson," Pierre reported in February.

"Yes?" Jean asked, affecting to be uninterested in the topic.

"He took his sweet time to respond to my bribe, so I shared some documents with his son-in-law. You know, the one who runs the New Orleans branch of the Second Bank of the United States."

"Pollock?"

"Yes. George Pollock. I let him understand that Spain has designs on Galvez Town, and that should we make a deal with the Spaniards, it would serve them as a very fine military station from which to launch attacks against New Orleans."

"And?"

"And lo-and-behold, a letter from Patterson arrived in less than a week. He will grant us a safe conduct pass to shield us from all American vessels, naval or revenue service alike, as long as we destroy our base here, and leave

170

American territorial waters for good, never to be seen again."

"That sounds ominous," Theodosia said. "Where would we go?"

"Anywhere but here." Pierre smiled. "I told him Venezuela."

"But you won't go to Venzuela, will you, Uncle Pierre?" Denise asked.

"We will go home," Jean said.

"*Home?!*" Theodosia and Denise chimed in unison.

"Where is home, Papa?" Denise asked.

"Home, Papa?" Glenn echoed.

"I thought we *were* home," Jules said.

"Home is Cartagena."

"Since when?" Theodosia asked.

"Since forever."

"Have you ever lived there, Jean?" Theodosia asked as if speaking to a very small child.

"No. Not yet. But it is home."

"I will leave you to your fantasies," Pierre said, laughing. "I just wanted to deliver the news myself. There are too many factors involved to entrust this information to a letter."

Jean almost tripped on the miniature wooden schooner on wheels that was lying unattended on the floor of the captain's cabin.

"Jean!" Theodosia ran to him, concerned, because she had never seen him stumble before. Was it the toy that nearly brought him down, or was he getting old? "Are you all right?"

"Yes. Just a little tired. I had to flog a man today."

"Oh."

"I haven't had to flog anyone in a long time, and I had forgotten how taxing it can be." He looked around as if in a daze. "Why are there so many wooden trinkets in here?" he asked, as if seeing the cabin for the first time in years. "I don't remember paying for any of this."

"Frank gave them to the children."

"Why?"

"Because... he likes to whittle."

Jean's brow started to furrow, as if he were smelling a rat. "I have never known anyone to do anything for free, unless there was something else he wanted." His eyes lit on a giant doll house in the corner of the room. It looked like a manor house and inside there was delicate furniture, divans and bedsteads and credenzas and spitoons and tiny rocking chairs.

"Why would our boys want a doll house?"

"It wasn't for them."

He turned to look at her. "Theodosia, are you trying to induce me to build you a house on the shore?"

"No, of course not."

"But you do want a house on the shore?"

"No, Jean. That house is not for me."

"Well, who is it for?"

"Denise."

"Denise?" He scratched his head. "She is too old to play with dolls."

"Yes. And not too young to long for her own house on the shore."

Dimly, the idea began to dawn on him.

"Now, Jean, don't get angry!"

"If he has laid one hand on her...!"

"He hasn't, Jean."

172

"How do you know?"

"Because I have been serving as their chaperone."

"Why would you do that?"

"Because... I care about your happiness, and you care about Denise."

"You knew I would not approve."

"Yes. That's why I didn't tell you."

"Then this is insubordination."

"I suppose it is." She stood her ground. "Are you going to flog me?"

He thought about it. "No. My arm is sore. Maybe tomorrow." And he sat down on the bed, defeated.

"Is Frank a good man, Jean?"

"Yes, he's a very good man."

"Then he would never hurt Denise."

"Not intentionally. But... she deserves so much better."

"What do you mean?"

"He's just a carpenter."

Theodosia laughed. "And you are just a sailor!"

"No. No, I'm not."

"Do you mean that you want her to marry one of your captains? A privateer?"

"No, I want nothing of the sort. I intentionally kept her away so that she would have no contact with my captains."

"Well, then what do you want for her?"

"A scholar."

She burst out laughing. "A scholar!"

"Yes. I promised my grandmother on her deathbed that Christina's children would have the best. That I would not make them follow in my footsteps or endanger their lives. That they would take a better path and live by the pen and not by the sword. I sent Antoine and Lucien to the best of schools. Nobody knew they were my sons. I gave them a good education. And Denise..."

"You kept her in that sordid little convent school."

"I wanted her safe."

"But it wasn't safe, was it?"

"No. But to marry her off to a carpenter? Can't you see, Denise is intelligent and sensitive and..."

"And Frank is an artist."

"Is he?"

"Look. Look at this portrait he whittled for her."

He looked at it for a long time. It was only a small, square piece of wood with no paint and no varnish, its edges sanded smooth. The face of a young girl was carved into it in subtle little grooves. It was the exact likeness of Denise, all the way down to her stubborn, mischievous expression.

"Yes, he is an artist," Jean said gravely. "I had not realized. I only ever had him build me rough hewn houses and a gallows." Then he asked: "How can he protect her?"

She laughed. "How would a scholar protect her?"

"With alchemy..." His voice was soft, because now she had reached inside his shirt and was kneading his back.

"Maybe you could teach him, Jean," she said.

On New Year's Eve 1820 Jean held a party for his captains and their crews aboard the *Saragossa,* and all was revelry and good cheer. The strains of bawdy beer songs and the words of *Auld Lang Syne,* sung by James Campbell, reminded Theodosia sadly of the belated ball held after the Battle of New Orleans. Then, for one short moment, Jean had been a celebrated war hero, a patriot and an important man admitted into the highest circles, standing right next to

174

Andrew Jackson and Governor Claiborne. That was five — nearly six — years ago, and it was a time of rejoicing. Now there was nothing much to celebrate, except that they had survived yet another year as hunted outlaws. It did not matter that Jean had laid down the law and kept a grip on the more rapacious and murderous elements in his commune. At the end of the day there was nothing but drunken camaraderie to keep it all together.

"Where is Denise?" Jean asked Theodosia during a lull in the rounds of drinks, none of which he ever downed.

"In her cabin, following your orders. You forbade her to leave it, remember?"

"You think I was too harsh?"

"I think you are mistaken."

"And where is young Mr. Little?" he asked. "I don't see him here at all, though I made a special point of inviting him."

She laughed. "Not in her cabin, if that is what you are insinuating."

"How do you know that?"

"Because they would not do that."

"Why not? They're young and in love. Why wouldn't they do that?"

"Because she is afraid. And she won't let him in."

"She's afraid of Frank?"

"No. Not of Frank. Of herself."

"What are you talking about?"

"She hasn't recovered yet," Theodosia said. "I have served them as dueña, and I know."

"Do you remember when Hattie acted as your dueña?" he suddenly asked.

"How could I forget!"

"I hope you are a better dueña than she was," he

chuckled.

"I don't have to be," she said. "Denise isn't ready to trust herself with Frank. Not yet."

"Why?"

There was a commotion on the foredeck and a cry of "Assassins!"

Jean left Theodosia to push his way through the crowd. It was Philippe Orozco and Frank Little beside him. "Jean Marotte and seven of his men are on their way here. They are planning to assassinate you!" Orozco cried.

"How do you know this?"

"We were at Madame Victoire's tavern when they were fortifying themselves with liquor," Frank said.

Jean looked at him. He seemed a little off himself. "And you – what were you doing there, Frank?"

The younger man looked a little sheepish. "I was fortifying myself with liquor as well, Sir, though for another purpose entirely."

"They are planning to come here at night after the party is over, when everyone is sleeping it off."

"They said they were going to kill you in your sleep," Frank added.

"That isn't very sporting!"

"Jean!" Theodosia was at his elbow.

"Go back to the *General Victoria*," he ordered. "I will send someone to escort you. Make sure the children are safe."

"Yes, Jean."

"Frank, do you want to go with her?"

"No, Sir. I would like to stay here and fight."

Jean nodded and called for another escort.

⚜

At a late breakfast the next morning the story was told. "Mr. Hall, Monsieur Rigaud, Mr. Cochrane, Señor Orozco and I stood guard over the strong boxes and safes aboard the *Saragossa*. It was dark, and we heard nothing for a long time. I even started to doze off," Jean said. "James Campbell and Frank Little stayed awake just outside the cabin door. They heard footsteps and a door squeak. Campbell fired the first shot at Marotte, then Frank shot him, as well. The rest of us then woke up and finished the job with the other six assassins."

"What did you do with the bodies, Papa?" Jules asked.

And Glenn, who was just now entering an echolalic phase also asked: "...with the bodies, Papa?"

"We threw them into the ocean."

"But why didn't you hang them, Papa?" Jules insisted.

"No need to make a fuss," he replied.

Theodosia thought for a moment that Jean must be a little embarrassed at the whole incident. He was used to doing battle with men in broad daylight, not skulking about in dark corners to thwart would-be assassins. This was not his finest hour.

"Papa, did Frank conduct himself with honor?" Denise asked, almost timidly.

"Yes, my pet."

"Then..."

"Then ... what?" Jean asked pointedly.

"Nothing, Papa." She looked away.

"He also asked me for your hand in marriage," he added, smiling, "which took considerably more courage."

"And what did you say, Papa?"

"Say? What is there to say?"

"Did you consent?"

"I'm not the one marrying him, Denise. How could I consent?"

"I would never marry him if you did not approve, Papa."

"No? Well, that is reassuring. Since you have been meeting him secretly behind my back for the past year and exchanging tokens of your affection."

"I have learned my lesson, Papa. I will let you decide this time."

"Let me decide?"

"Yes, Papa. The decision will be yours and yours alone."

He sighed. "Do you love him, Denise?"

"Yes, Papa."

"*Why* do you love him?"

"Why?" She was at a loss for a moment. "He is very kind," she finally said, sounding uncertain.

"Kindness is a good trait." Jean said. "But... it is not a sufficient foundation for marriage. Nor is affection. According to your stepmother."

Father and daughter both looked at Theodosia just then, and she wished she could disappear into the deck, for she sensed it was not an attribution that did her credit.

"He is also... not a coward," Denise ventured.

Jean laughed. "No, he's not. But you can't expect to marry every man you meet who is not a coward, as there are rather many of those."

"Yes, Papa."

"Is there any attribute that you feel uniquely qualifies him to be your husband? That distinguishes him from all others?"

"No, Papa." She was crestfallen.

"No?!" He sounded disappointed.

"I cannot justify the choice, Papa, by resorting to logical argumentation. But if anyone had to be uniquely suited to marry another, then I fear no one could ever marry."

"Ah!" he exclaimed. "Now we are getting somewhere. Why do you want him, Denise? Is it a matter of affection alone?"

"No, Papa. I also feel something else."

He leaned forward. "Do you feel... *passion?*" The intensity of the fire in his dark eyes alerted all present to the thin ice on which she was currently skating. All held their breaths.

"No, Papa," she answered meekly, her gaze averted and cast downward. "I have not felt passion with Frank. But..." and here she raised her coal black eyes again and met his glance almost defiantly: "But I *do* feel a terrible longing!"

He laughed. "Good answer."

No sooner had the betrothal of Denise Laffite to Frank Little been officially announced than James Campbell came running up with far more urgent news. "There's a warship out there, Jean, just past the sandbar!"

"Is it a Spanish vessel?"

"I can't tell. I will have to row out to see."

It turned out to be an American ship of war, and its captain in due course boarded a dinghy and came ashore, in the company of some of his men.

"Is Commodore Laffite anywhere hereabouts?" he asked, speaking to no one in particular, as all eyes were upon him. His smart naval uniform, consisting of a blue jacket complete with epaulettes and matching trousers, a red vest and yellow buttons, and a cocked black hat, was in sharp contrast to the appearance of all around him. If he expected to discern rank by examining clothing, he must have been sadly disappointed. Men of all descriptions had swarmed to the docks to catch a glimpse of the intruder. Faces of all colors, white, yellow, black and brown, hatless, wearing caps or in colorful sombreros, were looking straight at him, with no small degree of hostility. They were on the docked ships, the brigs and schooners, and lining the nearby walkway that led to the water. No two looked alike, and none were dressed in such a way as to betray their rank or importance.

The naval officer repeated his query: "Is Commodore Laffite here?"

Jean, standing on the deck of the *General Victoria* and dressed in a smart blue frock coat, replied: "There is no Commodore Laffite here, but *I* am Captain Laffite."

"I see," the Navy man replied crisply, as if this reduction in rank were somehow to Jean's detriment. "I am Lt. Lawrence Kearny, captain of the *USS Enterprise*, and I have been sent here by Commodore Patterson to make sure that this port is evacuated as promised."

"You are very welcome here, Lt. Kearny," Jean called out. "Please come aboard and enjoy the hospitalities of the vessel, both you and your men. As it happens, we were celebrating a family matter, so there is plenty of food and wine for all."

Theodosia sat at the table at Jean's side as dish upon succulent dish was served, and it surprised her to catch many of the officers frankly appraising her, as if she were one of Jean's possessions, and the quality of her beauty might reflect upon his prowess, much like the caliber of the cannons aboard his ship. Though it was warm inside the cabin, she drew her shawl tightly around her, because she had never known American men to behave so rudely. But Jean did not apear to notice.

"I am making arrangements, " Jean said, "to leave the bay. The ballast of the brig has been shifted. As soon as we can get over the bar, Captain, we sail."

"I had supposed that your flotilla was larger," Kearny interjected, in a manner that was almost insolent.

Jean disregarded this remark, and continued smoothly. "I have men on shore who are destroying the fort. Do you wish to inspect the proceedings?"

"In due time," Kearny replied. He seemed to be savoring his meal.

"I see you are enjoying the wild turkey," Jean remarked smiling. "It was cured in the sun, you see. That is what gives it its delicate flavor."

At an adjoining table, Denise was entertaining the midshipman from the Enterprise by deftly quatering oranges with a very sharp knife and then drinking silent toasts with an empty glass. The young man was a little tipsy, and his manner toward her was not in the least gentlemanly.

Jean, noticing that things were going a little too far at the other table, cut his conversation with the American captain short, got up from the table and gave her a withering look, so that she immediately dropped her glass and followed him into the hall.

Theodosia excused herself as well, and arrived just in time to hear Denise's retort: "But, Papa, I was only helping you. I pretended to be unable to speak a single word of English, and you should have heard the things they said of us when they thought I could not understand!"

"That they have no self-control and cannot tolerate the drink does not excuse your behavior, Denise!"

"They think we are savages. They believe I am your quadroon mistress. And that Emma is your *other* quadroon mistress."

"So?"

"So... that is insulting. They think my skin is too dark. The midshipman was saying to the second lieutenant that I was a fair maiden to take as a prize home to his ship. Then he corrected himself and said not fair, but dusky! And they laughed!"

"What difference does that make?"

"And they were saying that you were rather more stout than tall! Olive skinned, like all brigands. He said he could recognize the Englishmen and Americans among your sailors a mile away, as Spaniards and Frenchmen are all swarthy. But he said they found you rather less exotic than they supposed. And they are disappointed that you do not at all resemble the blood thirsty pirate chieftain they expected you to be! With a hook and an eyepatch and false medals on colorful sashes pinned to your chest!"

He laughed. "Denise, you will never succeed as a diplomat if you persist in repeating every slight you hear. Go down to your cabin and toy with these poor fools no more, before I am forced to send your fiancé to discipline you with his belt."

"Frank would never dare!"

"Perhaps he is more courageous than you give him credit."

"Papa!"

"Be good!" He pointed a finger at her. *"Sois sage!"*

She made a face at him, before she flounced off in the direction of her cabin.

"Where is Frank?" Theodosia asked.

"As soon as I saw the Americans were coming, I sent

him to the fort to supervise its dismantling. We will ship the timbers and sell them for profit, so it has to be done right."

Returning to the table, he said: "Please excuse my distraction. Can I offer you some more brandy? No? Then perhaps coffee?"

"Captain Laffite, may I ask you a question?" Lieutenant Kearny said.

"But of course."

"As we were coming up the pass we saw a dead body, quite old by the look of it, a bloated corpse mouldering on the line, hanging from a gibbet."

"Oh, yes. That is George Brown. He was tried for piracy and robbery and theft and... he was found guilty by a jury of his peers and sentenced to hang by the neck until dead."

Kearny cleared his throat. "Well, he appears to be thoroughly dead by now. Hadn't you better cut him down? It could be a health hazard."

"It serves as an example to my men that I will not tolerate piracy."

Kearny looked confused. "But, if you'll pardon my asking, Captain Laffite, are you not a pirate by trade?"

"No. I am not." Jean's dark eyes sparkled. "Nor have I ever been. I am at war with Spain. I have been at war with Spain for over fifteen years now, and under a privateering license, I have legitimately preyed on Spanish vessels, just as you, Lt. Kearny, must surely prey on the vessels of your enemies."

"But haven't you also looted American ships – I mean, you and your captains?"

"No. I have the highest regard for the United States of America. I have been its ally from the start."

"But what about the Filomena?"

"The Filomena is a Spanish vessel owned by a subject of his Catholic Majesty, the King of Spain, one Lorenzo Bru. You can check the court records and see that I am correct."

"But there was American cargo on board."

"It is not the nationality of the cargo that matters. Only the ship."

"But you've attacked British vessels, too, have you not?"

Jean laughed. "Indeed, I have, Lt. Kearny, during the late war between your country and the Britannians. I was on your side, remember?"

Kearny looked confused. He was a very young man and already the War of 1812 was fading in his memory. "Yes. Yes, of course."

"I assisted at the Battle of New Orleans," Jean said modestly. "I provided the flints and the powder and the artillery and the men."

"I had heard that, actually," Kearny admitted. "I mean, some people say *you* are the hero of the Battle of New Orleans just as much as Andrew Jackson. But then after the president pardoned you, you went rogue."

"From my perspective, Lt. Kearny, it is your government that went rogue, when after I won them the war, they confiscated my property and then paid tribute with money that was mine to their new allies the British, instead of demanding reparations for the Sack of Hampton and the burning of the White House. From some of the talk I have heard among your men, one might suppose the Americans and the British to be fair skinned brothers, while all Frenchmen are reviled as having been derived of inferior stock."

"Who told you that?" Kearny asked, taken aback.

Jean chuckled. "I have my spies."

✻

In the end, it took nearly another three months to clear out of Galveztown. Kearny, who turned out to be not entirely unsympathetic to Jean's cause, gave him a two month extension, and this, along with a second visit from the *USS Enterprise* that lasted two weeks, bought enough time to sell off most of the valuables and to distribute the cash among all the men of the commune, each according to his contribution. Nobody who had served Jean came away empty handed. He even gave several of his vessels as parting gifts to some of his loyal lieutenants, James Campbell among them.

Denise and Frank were married, and set off on their honeymoon to St. Louis, where Frank planned to start a furniture-making business with his severance pay. It was a tearful farewell.

One by one, all of Jean's followers scattered, each going a different way. Pierre had already liquidated his holdings in New Orleans and would soon be waiting to meet Jean in Cartagena with a vessel of his own. For himself, Jean kept only the *General Victoria*, the *Saragossa* and the *Ciel Bleu*, and the crews that he needed to operate them.

In the end, it was only Jean, Theodosia, Jules and Glenn who stood on the shore, watching the last of the buildings burn down. It was four o'clock.

Jules had made a big pile of all the wooden toys Frank had given him, and he was burning them as well, as a childish gesture of solidarity. But he was not as sporting a loser as his father, and there were angry tears streaming down his face as he cried: *"Les Américains sont méchants! Il faut les détruire! Il faut brûler leurs maisons! Il faut brûler la maison blanche!"*

Theodosia, much taken aback, answered in English: "No, Jules, I am an American, and so are you."

"I don't care," he bawled. "They must hate Papa very much to ask that we burn down our own houses. Why does Papa not take an army to Washington and burn down their houses! It would serve them right!"

Theodosia sighed. But as Jean said nothing, only stood there and watched the flames lick at what remained of the last pieces of timber, she answered: "Hatred is not always reciprocated."

Jules, confused by this sentence, calmed down enough to ask: "What does that mean?"

And Glenn repeated: "Does that mean?"

Jean finally turned around and looked at his son and translated: *"La haine n'est pas toujour reciproce."*

But Jules still seemed mystified. It was a difficult concept to swallow.

Even after they boarded the *General Victoria* and were looking at the shore from the vantage point of a league away, the fires still burned. Four leagues out to sea, and the flickering flames on the shore looked like a glorious sunset.

Chapter Ten
Secrets of the Silver Rattle

They spent a few months in Mexico and arrived in Cartagena de las Indias in June of 1821. The water was a topaz blue and the sky clear and the waves had froth on them that shone brilliant in the sun. Pierre was already waiting for them there, and he had even picked out a little house by the shore for the family to stay in. It was a pueblo-style structure, its walls made of mud bricks and coated with dried earth and dung, but painted on the outside in bright azure with golden yellow trim, as if a very small child had picked out the brightest and most cheerful hues for a toy house. The roof was flat, and one could climb up on a ladder built into the outer wall made of metal rungs to the top of the house and look out to sea, with an unobstructed view for leagues and leagues all the way to the horizon.

"Isn't this the most beautiful sight you have ever seen?" Jean asked her, from the top of the house.

"Yes," she breathed, and for a moment it was the truth.

But then he said: "I know you have always wanted a house on the shore. This is where you will stay when I go out on missions."

"What do you mean?"

"I have secured a commission with the Columbian

Navy. Bolívar has just retaken Cartagena from Spain. He has decided to abolish privateering altogether, but … he is continuing to enlist the captains of armed schooners to further his cause. When I am assigned on a mission, this will be our new base."

"Our new base?" It was just an adobe hut, fit for a mestizo to live in, nothing more. It was pretty, but it could never be home. And its clay and dung interior could not replace the relative luxury that she had known as the captain's woman on board the *General Victoria*.

"It is clean, it is close to the docks, and you will be safe here," he said, his face darkening, as he saw the resistance in her eyes.

"I feel safe only when I am with you, Jean."

"Pierre will stay with you when I go on my first mission," he said. "He is not feeling well right now. These spells come and go, but he will help you with your shopping and the barter with the neighbors. Until your Spanish improves, that is."

"Until my Spanish improves! I can spell in Spanish better than you can."

"What good is that if you cannot speak it?"

"Jean, I don't want to stay here alone."

He did not bother to answer her, instead turning to Jules and asking, "Where is Bandito?"

"He's still down there with Glenn," Jules replied. "Neither of them has figured out how to climb the ladder yet."

"Then perhaps you should go down and keep them company."

"Yes, Papa."

Turning back to her, he said, "Theo, this is new to me, also. It is not what we are accustomed to, you and I. But it is what we have. Make the best of it."

"Well," she sighed, "at least you are not locking me up in a nunnery."

"Not yet!" he teased, while twining his arm round her waist. "I will ask Pierre to take the boys for a walk, so we can try out the bed."

She laughed. He was less adventurous now than he would have been eight years ago when they met, opting for the bed, rather than the rooftop. Secretly, this pleased her. She had had her fill of adventure long ago. Now she longed for respectability and security, discretion and privacy. She wished they could make love in the strong room on board the *Saragossa* every time, where her cries could be muffled from prying ears. It embarrassed her when her sons woke up in the night because of her.

In the evening, after dinner, Pierre shared the latest news from New Orleans. "I was there in May when they hanged DesFarges and Johnson and the others."

"They hanged them?" Theodosia asked. Somehow, she had not believed it would happen.

"Yes."

She looked from Pierre to Jean. The elder brother was a realist and the younger was a dreamer. When she tried to meet his eyes, he winced.

"I was at Maspero's when the word came down that they would hang," Pierre recalled. "There was a group of us there sympathetic to their cause. Some of the men said they would start fires all over the city, so as to distract the authorities, and maybe the officers and crew of *Le Brave* could be saved. But they were disorganized and rowdy and thoughtless, and when the day of the hanging came, there was only a handful of fires that could easily be put out, and a few scuffles, and some explosions of gun powder stores, but no last minute salvation. They were hanged off the yardarms of a revenue service cutter moored in the Mississippi opposite the Place d'Armes. DesFarges asked for a pistol to shoot himself, and when it was denied him, he tried to drown himself in the river to avoid hanging, but they fished him out still alive and hanged him all the same."

"I... I thought they would be pardoned," Jean said, struggling with the words.

"Why did you think that?" Theodosia asked.

"Because I sent Ed to Washington with the express purpose to obtain the presidential pardon. I paid him quite a lot, not just for his time and the travel expenses, but also for the *bribes* that it would require."

"Monroe took all our money," Pierre aid, "and in return for it, he gave a worthless reprieve for sixty days. Then he sent an executive order that DesFarges and Johnson and all the rest should hang. Their blood is on his head. It wasn't Judge Hall's fault this time. *He* was inclined toward clemency. But when the president says 'hang them', what can a District Court Judge do? Ed was tireless, filing motions till the very end. On May 16, he moved for a suspension of the presidential order, but it was carried out all the same on the 24th. One man only got a presidential pardon."

"Who?"

"John Trickhart. The jury recommended him for clemency, as he claimed he did not know that he had signed up with bloodthirsty pirates and had no intention of participating in the general murder, carnage and rapine that was occurring on board the *Filomena*."

Jean laughed. "Clever bastard. That's the one *I* would have hanged!"

"Isn't that the way of things? And guess what? They also hanged those men of George Brown's that you sentenced to die two years ago and were spared by Captain Madison of the *Lynx*. Hanged them the very same day, as if they were no better nor worse than DesFarges."

"That's American justice for you. Slow as a turtle and blind as a bat."

Theodosia was glum. She could not speak up for her country, but it bothered her to hear it disparaged within earshot of her sons. Her honor was in tatters, for she could not stand up for herself as a patriot, any more than she could keep from crying out like an animal when Jean took her within earshot of their boys. Am I really a traitor? she wondered. Why is it so hard to speak up for America?

"Papa, why did you send money to President Monroe? I would have taken an army to Washington and razed it to the ground and sown it with salt so nothing would grow there ever again, *and* I would have run my sword through his black heart and put his head on a pike!"

Pierre laughed. "That is more easily said than done, my brave little nephew."

And Jean sighed. "I don't have an army, Jules. I am all powerful on the sea, but on land I am powerless."

"But why?" the boy insisted.

"Because your father does not *want* to fight the Americans, Jules," Theodosia finally intervened. "Isn't that right, Jean?" she asked pointedly.

"Your mother is right," he assented, as if this were a handy way out of a prickly problem. "I have enough on my hands at the moment with my War against Spain."

"But why are you at war against Spain, Papa, when it is always the Americans who are thwarting you?"

Pierre chuckled. "Good question."

"Because Spain is evil."

"Evil!" Glenn repeated gleefully.

There was a very long silence. Such an absolute condemnation was hard for anyone to counter, and nobody seemed at all inclined to try.

Then Jules, ever persistent, spoke up again. "But what has Spain done that is so very evil?"

"Spain arrested my grandfather and my grandmother Zora and put them in dungeons and tortured and shamed them, until my grandfather's heart burst and he died. They would have done the same to my grandmother, but she had strong magic on her side, and at night her brothers, who were sailors came and bore her away from there, and she never returned. She gave birth to her only child, my mother, when she was still in flight from the Inquisition. She never returned to the home of her youth, but lived as a refugee on Santo Domingo, where my mother met my father and married him, and bore him eight children and died. I grew up on Saint Domingue, and my grandmother served me as a mother. She taught me the tongue of her homeland, and I spoke Spanish before French. Spain harried and harassed everyone that I have ever known. They encouraged and incited the slaves on Saint Domingue to rise up against their French masters and gave them arms to slaughter us with. When Cartagena became independent of Spain, my two eldest sisters and their husbands came to live here to enjoy the atmosphere of freedom and honor that the Carthaginian spirit inspired. But in 1815, Pablo Morillo, a Spanish butcher, laid siege to the city, and,when it capitulated, he killed everyone who was here, men, women and children, leaving only a few abandoned and dejected slaves alive. They raped the women and they burned the houses and they behaved like savages. And I swore that someday I would avenge them!"

"Is that why you sent DesFarges and Johnson to rape

the women on the *Filomena*, Papa?"

"Jules!" Theodosia cried.

"What?!" Jean seemed equally taken aback.

Pierre laughed and laughed and laughed.

"Nobody raped anybody on the *Filomena*," Jean finally said, annoyed. "I do not permit rape."

"But it said so in all the papers. It said they were about to be raped, and only the Americans saved them."

"The papers lied."

"But Uncle Edward said that everything written in the papers is true."

"Ed was jesting, Jules."

"He was?"

"Of course."

"Then... Does that mean that the crew of Gambi's ship did not cut off his head with his own bloody axe while he was resting on a spar?" Jules sounded disappointed.

"Oh, no. That is God's own truth," Pierre replied, smiling. "That is too *good* not to be true."

"Then how can you tell which things in the paper are truth and which are lies?"

"You have to use your common sense, Jules," Pierre answered smoothly.

But as common sense was not in high supply on his side of the bloodline, Jules still looked very confused.

⚜

Jean went off on his first mission at the end of the summer and returned a month later. It appeared to have been uneventful, and he brought Theodosia and Jules a present on his return. "A History of the United States of

America, suitable for school children." he said, handing her the book with a smile. "I know that you are anxious to pass on your American patriotic fervor to Jules, so I bought you a book you could teach him from."

"But I am not interested in the history of the United States," Jules complained.

"You will be once your mother has had her way with you. And besides, it is about time you had some book learning. Your mother will teach you history and English, and I will instruct you in Spanish, French, fencing and navigation."

"Yes, Papa," he answered glumly. It was not much of a present.

A letter from Edward Livingston had arrived with some newspaper clippings from before Jean left on his first mission as a Columbian naval officer. Among these, the most notable read as follows:

The Courier, March 19, 1821
We understand that a schooner named the Nancy Eleanor, *on board of which was Pierre Laffite, brother of the celebrated pirate of that name, left this port in a clandestine manner a few nights since. It is said that she had on board arms and a large number of men, and is supposed to be bound on a piratical expedition.*

"Is that true, Uncle Pierre?" Jules asked, after the clipping had been passed to every family member capable of reading. "Were you bound on a piratical expedition?"

"I am never bound on piratical expeditions, Jules," Pierre replied. "And I would not call any ship of mine the *Nancy Eleanor,* as it is a foolish sounding name."

"Yes, it sounds like a girl's name," Jules agreed.

"Well, I don't mind girls, do you, Jules?" asked Pierre, taking a puff on his cigar.

"I suppose they are all right."

Another clipping from *The Louisiana Advertiser* told of the taking of the American ship *Orleans* by an unidentifed pirate who left this note before departing with his spoils:

> *At Sea and in Good Luck*
> *Sir,*
> *Between buccaneers, no ceremony. I take your dry goods and in return, I send you a pimento; there, we are now even. I entertain no resentment.*
> *Bid good day to the officer of the United States and tell him I appreciate the energy with which he has spoken of me and my companions in arms. Nothing can intimidate us. We share the same hazards, and our maxim is: "That the goods of the earth belong to the strong and valiant."*
> *The occupation of the Floridas is a pledge that the course I follow is in conformity with the policy now pursued by the United States.*
> *Signed, RICHARD CŒUR DE LION.*

In Livingston's hand the following was scrawled on the clipping: "Everyone here is sure this was written by you, Jean."

"Jean, that's not good!" Theodosia exclaimed. "This directly has you connected with acts of piracy against the United States."

"That wasn't me."

"But no one will know that."

He shrugged. "I can't help it. It's José Gaspar. He keeps claiming to be me, every time he attacks a ship, he leaves a cryptic message à *la Laffite*. I cannot help it if pirates keep impersonating me. My style is unique and inimitable, yet still they try."

"But it can get you hanged one of these days!"

"First, they have to catch me."

⚑

One day in early October, Theodosia came home from the market with Jules, and Pierre was gone.

"Where's Uncle Pierre, Papa?" Jules asked, after searching for him everywhere.

"He has gone to visit his wife."

"What?!" Theodosia was quite alarmed.

"He's gone back to New Orleans to visit Marie."

"But he can't do that! He'll get captured! And I need him here, Jean."

"What do you need him here for? You're married to me."

She needed him to help draw water from the well. She needed him to dicker with difficult merchants. She needed him as a buffer between herself and an unfamiliar world she would never understand. And most of all, she needed him to take the children for a walk so that she and Jean could be alone together. But she couldn't say any of that.

"Well, isn't it right that a man should go to visit his wife?" Jean asked, in a reasonable tone of voice.

She punched him in the shoulder. "No, it's not right. A man should not go to visit his wife. He should *live* with his wife!"

⚑

It was a bright sunny morning, with almost no

196

clouds in the sky.

"Maman, why did you give me such a bad mark on my history lesson?"

"Because your answers were all wrong. Do it over. Get it right."

"I think I got it right the first time, Maman."

"Well, I think you didn't."

"Look at this answer. Why did you mark it wrong? 'George Washington was a great leader of men who was able to maintain dicipline despite the freezing cold and the hardships of Valley Forge.'"

"Is that what you think?"

"Yes, Maman. That's what it says in the book."

"Well, that's not what happened. The men wanted to rebel at Valley Forge. George Washington had a stiff manner, and he did not have the common touch at all. They said that he dined on steak while they had nothing to eat. He sent my f… He sent Aaron Burr to discipline the men. Aaron Burr faced a long line of angry men who were prepared to shoot their muskets at him, but he knew something they didn't. He had removed their cartridges the night before. When the ringleader gave the signal to fire, Aaron Burr drew his sharp sword against the rebel's musket arm and nearly severed it, and he bade him stand in line, and all the others fell into place. Aaron Burr crushed the rebellion without killing a single man. And the men never resented him for it, for they admired his courage. And do you think General Washington was grateful for his help?"

"Yes?"

"No! He resented it. Aaron Burr never rose above the rank of Colonel, never received a commendation despite his bravery in battle and never got a military pension. Meanwhile, Alexander Hamilton, who curried favor with

Washington, won the General's recognition and a plum position on Washington's cabinet once the war was over."

"But it says right here in this book that Alexander Hamilton was a good man who was killed in cold blood by Aaron Burr, because he was too much of a gentleman to fire first."

"Let me see that." She looked at it for a long moment. "Well, it's a mistake. That isn't right."

"It's not?"

"No. Alexander Hamilton wanted to devalue our money, establish a central bank, plunge us into eternal debt and enslave us to the Revenue Cutter Service, which he founded himself in order to tax the people. He thought putting heavy duties on tea would cure people of their love of luxury. Love of luxury! He ate many a time at my ta... I mean, at Aaron Burr's table, and let me tell you, he had a love of fine wine and good food such as you cannot imagine. Aaron Burr always ate frugally, but Alexander Hamilton was served the best meats and sweets at Burr's table."

"Then they were friends?"

"They appeared to be, because whenever Hamilton made a rude comment, Burr forbore to take offense. But all this while Hamilton wrote libelous articles under an assumed name, accusing Aaron Burr of unspeakable depravity, when it was he who was a lecherous debaucher of women. He was a sanctimonious prig, full of self-serving religiosity, a favor seeker, and he lusted after power! And one day he went too far, so that even Aaron Burr could not allow for his insolence. He accused Burr of something unspeakable! Time and again Burr asked Hamilton to retract his monstrous accusation, but Hamilton would not. So Burr had no choice but to silence him forever on the field of honor. Hamilton was a very bad shot. He didn't throw the duel. He shot first, aimed wildly and missed. He lost, plain and simple. And as for his deathbed religiosity, he did that only to blacken the name of Aaron Burr and glorify his own name."

"You seem to know a great deal about it, Maman."

"Well, of course. Every American should take an interest in the history of our country. And you are an American, too, Jules. I expect you to do better than this!"

"Well, how about this answer: 'John Adams was a temperate president who served as a voice of moderation.'"

"Moderation? He plunged us into an undeclared Quasi-War with France. When people complained, he passed and signed into law the Alien and Sedition Act, in order to stifle dissent. He was a very bad president and was booted out of office after a single term."

"By Thomas Jefferson, right?" Jules asked.

"Thomas Jefferson *and* Aaron Burr," she corrected him.

"Are you sure?" Jules started flipping through the history book. "I don't think Aaron Burr was one of the presidents."

"They tied for the presidency in the electoral college. Burr very kindly allowed Jefferson to be president first. In return, Jefferson was supposed to let him be president the next time. Then Jefferson did not choose Burr as a running mate the second time he ran, and he later declared Burr to be a traitor, just because Burr wanted to lead an army against Spain."

"He went to war with Spain? Like Papa's 'War against Spain'?"

"Yes, just like you father's 'War against Spain'. But Jefferson had him arrested before he could even set out. He wanted him hanged for a traitor."

Jules looked confused. "Then Thomas Jefferson must be a very bad man, but one cannot tell it from reading the history book. Surely, James Madison must have been a good president?"

"Jules, James Madison declared war against Britain, then very nearly lost that war. The White House was burned by the British, and he had to flee for his life. Your father won the most important battle of that war and even supplied gun powder and flints without which an American victory would have been impossible. But do you think Jemmy Madison ever commended your father for his service, offered him a commission in the United States Navy or a letter of marque against Britain or Spain? Do you think he returned to him the ships and the goods that Commodore Patterson plundered from him when your father provided him with important information about the British invading forces?"

Jules shrugged. "I'm guessing the answer is... no?"

"That's right. No."

"So how is that my fault, Maman?"

"What do you mean, Jules?"

"Why did you give me a bad mark just because all the American presidents were bad people?"

"I think you should study your history book better."

"But *how*, Maman? It does not say any of that in the book!"

"You have to learn to read between the lines." She said it very calmly. "Now go and redo your lesson."

"You are insane, Maman!" Jules suddenly blurted out. "It will never say what you want it to say in that book! I hate the Americans, because of what they have done to Papa! I will always hate them! And you hate them, too. You must, or you would not say such terrible things about all their great leaders!"

Jean, who had been listening in on this conversation while perusing the *Gaceta Cartagena,* came and cuffed Jules on the ear. *"Respecte ta mère!"* he admonished, then walked out, headed toward the shops, the newspaper folded under his arm.

Jules had tears in his eyes. "I don't see why I should respect you. *He* doesn't!"

Theodosia's head spun. She felt in a moment what a fool she had been. Jean must have seen how ineffectual she was at teaching their son, and now her ears burned at Jules' accusation.

"Jules, why do you say that? Of course, your father respects me."

"No, he doesn't. Or else he would not hurt you every night until you cry."

"Jules!"

But the boy ran out of the house, and Bandito followed him, and that left Theodosia all alone with Glenn, who was playing with Jules' silver rattle on the floor.

She laid her head on the table, wanting to weep, but no tears came.

"I will be gone for a couple of months. We ship off in a week. I am leaving you enough provisions and some gold and silver coins to last you at least six months, but I will return long before that runs out."

"Don't go!"

"Theo, of course I must go. I have spoken to the neighbors. They will keep an eye on you. I wish you would make more of an effort to speak to them. If you don't

201

practice your Spanish, it will never improve."

"I have tried to speak to them," Theodosia said. "I don't think those people *know* any Spanish."

He laughed. "And *you* are the one to judge?"

"No, honestly, I did! I spoke very plainly, and my pronunciation is not that bad. My tutor back in Charleston even said so. I spoke as plain as day. And they replied in something that did not sound like Spanish at all! I could not understand a word."

"Well, you can't expect them to speak Castilian. You should listen first and then imitate the way they speak. It's the only way to learn. Theirs is a Spanish creole. Most of the people here are abandoned slaves."

"Don't you mean freed slaves?"

"No."

"Or runaway slaves?"

"No. They are slaves who have lost their masters. They are like orphans. They were not freed, and they did not run away. Pablo Morillo killed everyone who was anyone, men, women and children, just because Cartagena dared to defy Spain. The only ones who were left were slaves too lowly to bother with. Now they have no one to take care of them, so they fend for themselves. But as they were brought here from Africa less than a generation ago, this is not their home. They are not natives and cannot return to the land. They don't know how best to feed themselves. The sack of Cartagena was as much a calamity for them as it was for their masters. Everyone was killed, and there was nothing to eat, and rotting corpses everywhere. That is why they are so poor. But they are good people, and they hate Spain just as we do. They will help you, if you need help. You have only to ask."

Theodosia was not interested in hearing how the

poor family next door hated Spain as much as Jean did. She was tired of that. Why he would lecture her on the importance of his lifelong vendetta when she needed him home with her, she could not understand. "There's going to be another baby," she whispered. "I don't want you to leave."

"Be reasonable. Of course, I have to leave. There is the war against Spain."

"You can't fight a one man war against Spain."

"It's not a one man war. There are others fighting, too. We are all fighting together to destroy Spain's tyranny."

"And replace it with what? Another tyranny? What is the point?"

"What was the point when I fought the Battle of New Orleans against Britain?"

"Jean, Britain was attacking us. The British were blockading our coastlines. They sacked and burned and pillaged and raped. I asked you to help me, because I wanted my country back."

"And now you have it."

"I *don't* have it," she sobbed. "It's far, far away from here, and I am homesick. The least you could do is stay with me."

"Isn't it right that I should want *my* country back, too?"

"What country?" She was confused. "Which is your country, Jean? Is it France? You want to go live in France? Fine. I'll live with you in France. I actually do speak French! It will be better than here."

"I can't go live in France. The monarchy has been restored. And anyway, it's not my country."

"Then is it Spain? You want to go back to Spain?"

"No, it's not Spain!" He spat the words out. "How could it be? I hate Spain with all my heart! My country is here."

"Your mother tongue is Spanish. Your grandmother was a Spaniard. You are always happiest when you are around people who speak Spanish. You and Antonio de Sedella were talking and laughing together about good old Cadiz back in New Orleans. I heard you. Do you think that I've forgotten? Why not go back to Spain?"

"Spain is evil, remember, Maman?" Jules interrupted. "All the Spaniards are evil."

For a moment Jean and Theodosia stopped bickering long enough to focus on their son. "Jules, that's not true," she said.

"Yes, it is. Papa said so."

"Is this really how you want to raise your son? Full of hatred for people he does not even know?"

Jean paused for a moment, his mouth half open. Then he turned away from her and looked down. "Jules, listen to me. It is not true that all Spaniards are evil," he said, kneeling down before the boy, meeting him at eye level.

"They're not?"

"No. My grandmother was a Spaniard. She was a very good woman."

"But you said... You said Spain was evil, so it must be the case that all Spaniards are evil, too. Otherwise, what would it mean that Spain is evil? How can a country be evil? Only *people* can be. So that means all Spaniards are evil."

"It is not true that all Spaniards are evil. Most Spaniards are good people, just as most Frenchmen are good people and just as most Americans are."

"But you said..."

"I said that Spain was evil! And I want to save all people, including the Spaniards, from its clutches. I want all men to be free."

"Even the slaves, Papa?"

"Even the slaves, in due course. But in order to make that happen, I must continue with my War against Spain."

Theodosia rolled her eyes. "How will you know when you've won?"

"I will know victory when I see it."

⚜

Glenn was on the floor playing with the silver rattle, and Theodosia was mending socks, when Jules came in and presented her with his lesson re-worked.

"Maman, I rewrote the answers the way you wanted," he said, handing her the sheets. "I mentioned Aaron Burr many times. His bravery. And how he was nearly president. Why do you like Aaron Burr so much, Maman?"

She sighed. "He was a good man, that's all. He was a good man, and they wronged him." She took the assignment from him, not bothering to glance at it. Then she took him by the arms and looked into his eyes and said: "Jules, I don't hate my country. I am *not* a traitor. You do know that, right?"

"Yes, Maman. I know you love your country. Just as Grandmother Zora *must* have loved her country, too. But Papa still wants to avenge her by destroying Spain. Because that's what men do for the women they love. Women are weak, so they need men to go to war for them. I know you love your country, and you only hate the people who are in charge. And someday, when I grow up, I will avenge you. I will bring you President Monroe's head on a plate."

"No! Don't do that, Jules! I don't hate anybody. And I don't want President Monroe's head on a plate."

"You don't?"

"No."

"Well, what do you want, Maman?"

"I want them to change what it says in that history book. Because it's not true. But I don't hate anybody."

He shuffled his feet. Finally, he said: "You don't have to lie to me about that, Maman. I know you hate President Monroe, because he ordered us driven away and our houses burned. And because he ordered DesFarges hanged, when everyone in New Orleans hoped he would be pardoned. And because the Navy is out hunting for Papa, and they're going to hang him, too, if they catch him. You must hate President Monroe just a little for that. Anyone would! It's all right."

"I don't, Jules. I don't hate anyone. I'm just a little tired, that's all."

"Maman, I know you're sad because Papa is leaving, and you are afraid here. But you don't have to be. I will take care of you. I can speak to the neighbors and bargain for you at the market and draw the water from the well. And I will be kinder to you than Papa is."

"Jules, your father is not unkind to me."

"He hurts you. He makes you cry out."

"No. No, he doesn't. That is a cry of joy, Jules. When you are older you will understand. Sometimes there is so much sorrow in life, and there is only one way to gain a little respite from it. Your father helps me forget."

"What do you want to forget, Maman?"

"Nothing." She turned away to tidy the table, which was covered with the socks she had been darning, so she could spread out the papers he had given her and begin to read.

Glenn pointed the silver rattle at Jules, but when Jules tried to take it away, he drew it back, and said: "Mine!"

"No, actually it's mine," Jules said. "It was given to me

by … our grandfather, AB. See, it says that right here. To JJL from AB."

"AB?"

"Yes. I used to think it meant *abuelo*. But now I am beginning to suspect that it might stand for something else."

Chapter Eleven
The Heliograph

Before he left, Jean took Theodosia and Jules up to the top of the house and said: "I have a present to give you."

"What is it?" asked Jules, staring at the red pouch.

"It is a heliograph."

"A sun writer?" Theodosia asked.

"Yes! You've heard of it?"

She sighed. "No, Jean. I merely parsed the word. It's Greek, you know."

"Well, this is the latest advance in long distance communication, and I have got one, too. It captures the light of the sun and can send it to people far in the distance, as far as the eye can see. It will send out messages at the speed of light. When I am away at sea, we can still speak to each other in cipher. If you climb up to the roof, there will be no obstructions even when I am leagues away."

And he took out the curious looking glass and metal object from its velvet pouch and proceeded to teach his wife and son the code that turns the miles to naught. "You choose your target by aiming the crosshairs here, and then you interrupt the flash of light by tilting the mirror. And now I will teach you the cipher that we will use, that no one else will know."

They practiced for many hours.

"We will never be truly apart," he said to her, and Theodosia, caught up in his enthusiasm for the new invention, began to believe.

At first, after he left, it was true. They would send each other messages every day. But in time the messages grew fewer, and eventually they stopped. And two months passed, and he did not return.

⁂

The neighbors kept smiling and waving at her every time that she passed. "Señora Laffite!" they greeted her, and she tried to reciprocate, although in truth she had trouble remembering their names and had no idea what they were saying every time they stopped to converse.

"I wish they would not bother trying to talk to me," she muttered, as she hauled the heavy basket from the market. "It only confuses me."

"Papa asked them to do that, Maman. He was worried that you would be lonely here once he was gone."

"Well, he needn't have bothered. I'm perfectly capable of keeping myself entertained in his absence."

"You're angry with him?"

"No. Of course, not. I am just ..." She nearly stumbled.

"Here let me take the basket, Maman."

"It's too heavy for you, Jules. You're still just a little boy."

"Maybe if you balanced it on your head like all the other women..."

She glared at him. "I wasn't raised to do that, Jules!"

The house was up on a hill, the better to view the ocean, but this made carrying things home from market twice as hard. And she was getting heavier, though it was only three months along.

"Just keep your eye on your brother, Jules."

"Don't worry, Maman. Bandito is watching him. He won't let him lag behind us." In fact, Bandito had taken on the job of herding the entire family, gently nudging any stragglers.

When they approached the house, Bandito began to bark.

"There's someone inside, Maman."

"Maybe it's your father. Maybe he's returned."

"He would not bark like that at Papa."

Theodosia hurried into the house. The idea of a thief or an intruder did not even occur to her. There were no locks on the doors here, and the windows were always open. Nothing of real value was stored in the house, and what few coins remained of their budget were secreted on her person.

"Madame Laffite," he said. "I hope you will not mind the intrustion."

"Père Antoine!" Jules cried out from behind her.

The priest dressed in a monk's garb hurried to relieve her of the basket that she was carrying and ceremoniously deposited it on the table. Then he pulled a chair for her to sit in. "Please be seated. It is with a heavy heart that I must share this news with you."

Stunned, she let herself into the chair, unable even to resist. "What is it?"

"It is with regard to your ... husband, shall we say?"

"Jean? What about Jean?"

"I do not wish to alarm you..."

"Is he dead?" For a moment, she was certain he must be. Jean would not let that man into their house, would not force her to bear one more moment of his slithering machinations. Jean had banished him from Galveztown.

210

Their association had been over years ago.

"Dead? No. Not yet. But he has been captured. And they have him in custody, and in due course he will be taken to New Orleans to stand trial."

"No!"

"Oh, yes. I thought, since I am already in town on other business, I might offer you a berth on my ship, you and your children, of course, as you will no doubt want to be there when he is tried, and will wish to say your adieus before the hanging."

"No!" Everything was going black. She could barely focus on the priest, or the two men standing behind him, or the other two men in yard that she saw through the window behind them.

"Maman, he's lying. He doesn't have Papa! He would not come here if he did. It's a trap."

"Jules, please," de Sedella said. "I'm your friend. Don't you remember me?"

"Yes, I remember you. I don't like you, anymore, Père Antoine. Not since you cursed us with the great storm."

"What?"

"Leave Maman alone."

"Jules, be quiet," Theodosia said, her head still spinning.

"He doesn't have Papa. He could never capture him!"

"Well, *I* have not captured him, young man. I never said I did. It was the United States Navy that did that. I just happen to have heard about it. And upon learning that you have made your residence here, I thought I would offer you and your mother and your little brother safe accomodations for the trip back to New Orleans." He turned to Theodosia and offered her his arm. "Here, let us not delay. The ship is waiting."

She swatted his hand away. "No. No, I'm not going with you."

"But there are orders that you are to come."

"I don't take my orders from you. I only take orders from Jean."

"He is not your husband."

"No. But he *is* my captain!"

"Please think carefully, Madame," de Sedella said very softly. "Consider your position. Your father could still be deeply embarrassed if it were known that you have served as a pirate's whore all these years. And should they link his treason to yours... "

"Leave!" she shouted. "Leave here at once!"

"I must insist that you come with me," he replied calmly and started to reach for her arm. Theodosia could not even feel her body. She felt light as air, and she had a remarkable tunnel vision that allowed her to focus on the priest to the exclusion of all else. She did not know what was happening, but her hand reached for the nearest object on the table, which happened to be a carving knife, and she plunged it into his chest.

The wound must have been a shallow one, for he took the knife from her, as if her wrist had been made of straw, and, looming over her, he said: "That, Madame, was a mistake."

"Drop the knife, Père Antoine!"

She looked behind her. Jules was leveling a musket at the priest.

"You wouldn't! Think about your soul."

"I *am* thinking about my soul!"

Bandito growled, then there was a cry from the priest. "May God damn you!" de Sedella intoned, almost as if it were a blessing.

She heard the knife clatter to the table, then spun around to see the priest running out the door, the dog latched on to his heels, and Jules after him, followed by little Glenn. The other men took off, too. Theodosia fished for the heliograph in the velvet pouch. She climbed to the top of the roof. Down below, she could see an army of brown little children chasing the priest and his henchmen down the hill, throwing rocks at them all the way. She did not understand how they had been summoned, but Jules and Glenn and Bandito were there on the periphery of the assault, and all the way down the road to the shore new little brown figures were springing forth, joining the fray.

She set up the heliograph and tried to signal Jean. He had not been captured. She was sure of it. The priest had merely been trying to kidnap her. But no answer came back no matter how many times she tried to raise him, and in time, she gave up.

She went downstairs and threw herself down on the bed, sobbing. And that's when the pains began.

When Jules looked in on her an hour later, she was lying in a pool of blood.

"Maman!"

"Fetch the midwife," she said. She did not even know if there was a midwife in this godforsaken place. But it was all she had the strength to say.

✻

The next day or so was a blur. A woman came and nursed her. The remains of the baby were buried in the yard. She slept. She wept. She slept some more.

When she felt fully recovered, she found her two boys sitting at the table eating something savory-smelling out of earthen bowls.

"Where did this food come from?"

"The neighbors. Do you want some, Maman?" Jules got up with alacrity and filled a bowl for her.

She sat down to eat. "They know how to cook, these neighbors of ours," she said. "What is it?"

"Pig's ear stew," he replied.

She laughed. "It tastes better than it sounds." She was famished and full of energy. The little parasite who had been draining her strength was gone, and now she could move mountains.

"Maman, this arrived in the post. It's for Papa."

She ripped it open. It was a letter from Edward Livingston, and with it a single clipping from *The Courier*.

> *We have been informed that the famous Laffite of piratical memory, after having been wrecked on the island of Cuba, being destitute of all means of living, and of escape, had been discovered and apprehended by some inhabitants, who brought him to Porto Principe, where he was thrown into a dungeon. Unfortunately for mankind, Laffite was recognized by several influential persons of the place, to whom he formerly rendered some service, and who facilitated his escape. We cannot avoid applauding the feeling of gratitude which moved these persons to break the chains of their benefactor, but at the same time we cannot too deeply regret that the monster who has shed so much innocent blood, should have, perhaps for the hundredth time, escaped the sword of Justice, which has so long been hanging over his guilty head.*

On the edge of the clipping, Livingston, in his unmistakable scrawl had written: "Close call!"

"You see, Maman, there is no need to worry. He has escaped. I knew he would!"

"But this cannot be what de Sedella was talking about," Theodosia said to Jules. "He said a Navy vessel had him."

"But he lied."

"No, Jules, I don't think he did. If your father were at large, he would have come home to us by now, or he would have sent word. But I cannot raise him on the heliograph, and all contact has been severed. It therefore stands to reason that he has either been captured or is dead."

"No, Maman!"

"Yes. If dead, then this presents no problem."

"No problem, Maman?!"

"I mean, we cannot raise the dead, and there is nothing whatever to be done about it."

"Yes, Maman, but..."

"If he's alive, on the other hand, then we must try to help him."

"Yes, Maman."

"If what de Sedella says is true, and they are taking him to New Orleans to be hanged..."

"I don't think that is true, Maman."

"If it is true, then we must use every means at our disposal to ensure that he does not hang."

"Yes, Maman."

"We will... We will hire a sharpshooter." She said it with great conviction.

"A sharpshooter?" Jules sounded dubious.

"Yes. A sharpshooter, such as they use for assassinations. And when your father is brought out on the revenue cutter, there will be a clear shot."

"At the hangman?"

"No, Jules. At your father. One clean shot and he will be dead. And they won't be able to hang him, the way they did DesFarges."

"Maman!"

"Jules, don't worry. Your father will not hang. I will not allow it!" She felt very satisfied with herself and started tidying the kitchen. But for some reason Jules kept looking at her as if she were insane.

⚜

All day she cleaned the house like a madwoman, until everything sparkled. Then she went out into the yard and swept the dirt, until her glance fell on the newly dug grave. And then she collapsed on the ground, sobbing, and the fresh dirt mingled with her tears.

But Jules was on the roof of the house fiddling with the heliograph, and presently he came down and hugged her and said: "Don't cry, Maman. It's all right. I spoke to Papa just now. The Americans *do* have him, but they are not taking him to New Orleans. They are bringing him back here, to Cartagena."

She wiped the dirt from her eyes. "Why would they do that?"

"Because he has friends on board who do not want him to hang. You see, it's going to be all right!"

"Friends on board!"

"Yes, Maman. Uncle Arsène is aboard that ship. You know he is enlisted in the American forces, don't you?"

"Yes, but..."

"And there are still others who served with him in the Battle of New Orleans. They were comrades at arms. They will not turn him in to be hanged."

"But they have orders from the President."

"To arrest him, Maman. Which they have. But they will turn him over to the authorities here. And he will not stand trial in New Orleans."

"But how do you know this is true?" she asked.

"It is Papa's very own words in our private cipher."

"But they could have tortured him and gotten the code."

Jules smiled. "No, they didn't."

"How do you know? Why are you so certain?"

"Maman, you know how Papa has his own special way of spelling things, even in French, which is different from the way any other person spells them?"

She nodded. His spelling was a great source of embarrassment to her.

"Well, nobody else could have written those words but Papa!"

She laughed. "Oh, thank goodness for that." And she hugged Jules tightly.

Chapter Twelve
The Obituary

It was not until the end of May, 1822 that the word was given that Jean Laffite was indeed in Cartagena. A Captain Richard Stockton of the *USS Alligator* paid a courtesy call on Theodosia with a message from Jean. Stockton had turned Jean over to the local authorities, and now he was a prisoner in the citadel. By then Theodosia's funds were running very low, and she was grateful for frequent gifts from the neighbors, who without seeming to be charitable, contrived to bring leftovers from their meals to share with the wife and children of the famous Laffite.

Day after day, Theodosia and Glenn and Jules went to the city to inquire when Jean would be released. The answer was always *mañana*.

"He said that yesterday and the day before," Theodosia complained to Jules, who was acting as interpreter. "Jean is a commissioned Colombian naval officer. Why do they have him imprisoned at all?"

"The Americans charged him with piracy, Maman, and Gran Colombia is at peace with the Americans. Bolívar has even outlawed privateering, because he wants to please the Americans and show that his government is legitimate. So the local authorities are investigating the charges. When they discover that Papa is not a pirate, they will let him go."

The guard at the front desk viewed them impassively, shuffling papers. He did not understand a word they were saying.

"Well, couldn't they investigate faster?" she asked, looking at the guard, who was openly staring at her.

"Maman, I don't think you understand how things work in Gran Colombia."

"Really? How do things work?"

"I think that man wants us to give him some money."

"Did he say so?"

"No, Maman. But I am reading between the lines."

She gave him an odd look. He had matured so much in the past year. "I don't have much money left, Jules."

"I know, Maman. But I have something." He drew the silver rattle from his pocket.

"No, Jules! That's yours. It was a gift from your grandfather."

"I don't need it, anymore, Maman. It has served its purpose."

As soon as the bribe was proferred, the wheels of justice moved much more speedily. By the end of the workday, Jean was released.

⁂

He had lost weight, and he walked with a limp, but his spirits were high and his bravado undiminished. He hugged Theodosia and kissed her cheek, and his strong musk from days and weeks and months of incarceration made her feel at once both safe and bitterly nostalgic, longing to be alone with him, but fearful lest he might have changed. She wanted to stay in his embrace forever, but the boys were clamoring for his attention.

"Papa! Papa! Tell us about your travels!"

And little Glenn showed him his finger. "I stubbed it."

Jean reached down and kissed the finger, and she wanted so much to tell him that she had lost the baby, but she held back, because it was not the right time.

"First we will visit the bank, then a bath house and afterwards have a nice festive meal at the cantina," Jean said.

"Do you keep money in this bank?" Theodosia asked, as he was writing out a draft.

"Oh, no. I would never keep money in an establishment as unstable as this one. I am simply drawing a draft on my Swiss account. They know I am good for it."

The bath was taken in a barbershop, while he was shaved. Theodosia and the boys stood and watched. Then it was off to the cantina. At the meal, which all ate with great gusto, Jean told them about his adventures. At least, to the boys, they seemed like adventures. To Theodosia, it was nothing but an unremitting series of calamities and near escapes. And yet he sounded so cheerful in the telling.

"I took on a rather large cargo vessel off the southern coast of Jamaica. It was smaller than a schooner, but much larger than a sloop. But instead of striking her colors, she fought back."

"When was that, Papa?"

"Soon after I set out. About a month after I left here. Still we took the prize, and though one of my men was killed, and two were wounded, it was a good fight. I held the prize for two days, and then I ransomed her to her owners, who agreed to make payment in Cuba."

"Where in Cuba, Papa?"

Jean was reenacting the battle with salt shakers and salsa dishes, and he said: "Right here, near Santa Cruz del Sur," and he pointed at a large bowl full of tortillas that was standing in for Cuba. "When we approached the port, two armed Spanish vessels came out of the harbor. We had not been counting on that!"

"What did you do, Papa?"

"Well, we did our best. But we were outnumbered and outgunned. They retook the prize, and in the end, they killed most of my men and boarded my ship."

"The *General Victoria*, Papa?"

"Oh, no, Jules. The *General Victoria* has been sold for some time now. I gave her and the *Saragossa* to your Uncle Pierre to resell in the ship market off St. Barthélemy months ago, before he went on to New Orleans. The proceeds have safely been deposited in my Swiss account."

"But why, Papa?"

"Because when Bolívar retook Cartagena from Spain, in October, he announced that he was nationalizing all privateering vessels."

"What does nationalizing mean, Papa?"

"It means they become the property of Gran Colombia, instead of the original owners."

"But that's awful, Jean!" Theodosia exclaimed.

"Yes, well." He shrugged. "I was not going to lose two of my vessels without payment, so I sold them before it was too late. But I willingly contributed the *Ciel Bleu* to the national fleet in return for a commission in the Colombian Navy."

Theodosia snorted. "Willingly contributed? Did you have a choice?"

"Yes, my love. We always have a choice. I could have taken all my vessels and left. But since serving in Bolívar's navy affords me an opportunity to continue with my war against Spain, I chose to stay and fight."

"So it's the *Ciel Bleu* you lost, Papa?"

"Yes, Jules. But technically it was not I who lost it, since I no longer owned it. The loss was that of Gran Colombia."

"Then what happened?"

"The Spaniards boarded my vessel and arrested me."

"But why didn't they hang you, Papa, right then and there?"

"Ah. Well, there is a thing that the Spaniards love to do. They consider themselves a nation of laws, instead of men. They wanted me properly tried and chastened, tortured and humbled, and made an example of, and all that it entails, so they cast me into their brig, from which, of course, I escaped at once."

"Of course!" Jules exclaimed. And Glenn, happy to be a part of it all, clapped his hands.

Theodosia shook her head in despair.

"Were you alone, Papa, when you escaped?"

"No, several of my men came with me. We swam all the way to Santa Cruz de la Sur, which admittedly was not very far off. We had no food and no arms and no money, and when we asked for help of the local inhabitants, they did not recognize us as liberators, and they turned us over to the Spanish authorities."

"And why didn't they hang you then, Papa?"

"It is a peculiar weakness of the Spaniards that they have a very powerful bureaucracy, and they are devoted to the letter of the law. Nobody can be hanged there without having all the proper documents signed in triplicate. So they took us several miles inland to the provincial capital of Porto Principe."

"And there they threw you into a dark dungeon?"

"Well, there is no need to exaggerate. It was just a jail."

"The papers said a dungeon!"

"You know how the papers like to sensationalize everything, Jules."

"Yes, Papa."

"After a few weeks in the jail, my wound got much worse."

"What wound?" Theodosia asked, alarmed.

"Oh, didn't I mention I was wounded?"

"No, Papa."

Seeing Theodosia's worried face, Jean said. "Well, it was really just a scratch, nothing to be concerned about, but it began to fester, and I became a little feverish, so the cunning Spaniards decided to move me to the hospital of San Juan de Dios, just as a precaution."

"Why did they do that, Papa, if they are so evil?"

"Simple. They wanted to give the appearance of being kind and merciful. They wanted me to be in the best of health when they finally hanged me."

Theodosia rolled her eyes.

"Of course, I took this opportunity to escape again."

"Of course."

"I hurried back to the coast. I went directly to Cayo Romano, where, as everybody knows, there is a well established community of freedom fighters. They operate out of the Old Bahama channel, mostly going after slavers. I made a deal with one of them, and in no time at all I was the captain of a schooner."

"Really, Papa!" Jules' eyes were brimming with admiration.

"Soon I commanded a fleet of not one but four corsairs. I was the captain of the *Cienago* and had three other ships under me. On April 11, I took an English sloop. Unfortunately, there was an American Navy vessel in the vicinity, and the Americans and the British have become rather chummy of late."

"It was the *Alligator*, wasn't it, Papa?"

"Yes, Jules. Commanded by Captain Stockton. Since I have sworn never to fight the Americans, I had to strike my colors. They took my ship and arrested me."

"And then what happened, Papa?"

"And then we had a party!"

"What?!"

"It just so happened that my old friend, Arsène Latour was on board, as well as several veterans from the Battle of New Orleans. They toasted my health! They sang *Auld Lang Syne* and *For He's a Jolly Good Fellow*. I was treated to the best dinner I had had in a long time. And in the end – in the end they brought me here. Of course, as they could not be seen to be releasing a wanted pirate, they turned me over to the Colombian authorities of Cartagena. But they never would have brought me back to New Orleans to hang!"

On the walk all the way back to the azure colored house on the hill, Jean and the boys were chattering happily, but inside something began to eat away at Theodosia.

When they were finally alone that night, with the boys camped out on the other side of the bedroom door, she pummeled him. "You had a party?!"

"What's wrong with that?"

"I thought you were dead. I thought... I thought it was over! I stabbed de Sedella with a carving knife! I lost the baby! I nearly died. We have been starving for months. And *you* had a party!"

"You stabbed de Sedella with a carving knife? Why on earth would you do that?"

"Because you weren't here to do it for me!"

"I have never stabbed anyone with a carving knife,"

Jean protested. "I would never do that. It is very poor form." Then he remembered to ask. "What was de Sedella doing here?"

"He came to tell me that you had been arrested and were to stand trial in New Orleans, and he wanted to escort me to the hanging." She told him everything that had happened.

"He was probably hoping to work out a deal for my extradition," Jean said. "I am sorry he bothered you."

"Bothered me? I lost the baby!" And her face crumbled into isolated pockets of whimpering, and then she began sobbing.

He held her tight and let her cry it out. Then when all had passed and even the hiccups were gone, he made her look up at him and wiped away the tears. "I lost my ship," he said softly, caressing her hair. "Many men died who served under me. I barely escaped with my life."

She looked up at his face and saw past the bluster and the bravado. And she forgave him. And when, in due course, after passion had been sated, she chanced to observe the dreadful scar on his thigh, she said a silent thank you to the cunning Spaniards who had spared his life and sewn him up and nursed him back to health.

Jean spent days upon days visiting all the neighbors and bringing them presents and thanking them for their help. Then he went back into town, and after only half a day, he announced: "I have a new ship!"

"You bought a new ship, Papa?"

"No, I have been *assigned* to a new ship belonging to the Colombian fleet. It is called the *General Santander*, after

Francisco José de Paula Santander y Omaña, the hero of the Granadan revolution, and the current acting President of Gran Columbia."

"I thought that was Simon Bolívar," Jules piped up.

"Well, Bolívar is our president, but he is a very busy man, seeing as he has to lead the military campaigns in Ecuador and Peru against the forces of the Spanish royalists. So he has left his very good friend, General Santander, who is the vice president, to be acting president in his absence."

"I hope they are better friends than Thomas Jefferson and Aaron Burr were," Jules mused.

"I am sure that they are. Anyway, I sail next week, so I expect you to continue with your navigation studies in my absence and help your mother with anything that she requires of you."

"Yes, Papa."

"Don't go, Jean," she said very quietly, but her eyes were pleading.

"Of course, I must go."

"You were lucky this time. Next time they will catch you and hang you Don't go!" She came and twined her hands round his neck. "Please!"

"Do not *you* be the noose round my neck!" he bristled, and, tearing himself from her embrace, walked away.

At breakfast on the day before the launch, Theodosia was woodenly going about her duties, when Jean joked, "Let's hope your mother has not poisoned my meal as an expedient to prevent me from being hanged."

Jules laughed.

"It would serve you right!" she said.

"Why would it serve me right? And what were you thinking, wanting to hire a sharpshooter to kill me in the event that I was sentenced to hang?"

"Jules told you about that? Well, he shouldn't have."

"Theodosia, do you think that I am not capable of conducting myself with honor in the event of a hanging? Did you think I would not die bravely?"

"I don't want you to die at all, but if you must die, do it any other way! I will not have it said that you were hanged like any common horse thief."

"This is what concerns you? What people will say?" His voice was stern and merciless.

"It is not an honorable death."

"Any death is an honorable death when faced with courage."

"I could not bear for you to hang."

"Of course, you could. If I am hanged, I expect you to be in the front row, cheering me on."

"No!"

"No? That is your duty as my wife."

"You cannot force me. I refuse."

He got up and stormed out, and in the evening he returned and dangled some papers in front of her face, all tied with a ribbon. "I have thought about what you said. You are right. I cannot force you to attend my hanging. And if you do not wish to be there, then it can only mean one thing, that you do not wish to be my wife. Because we swore – do you remember? – that we would accompany one another all the way to hell if necessary..."

"If necessary, Jean! But why is it necessary?"

"You have known about my war against Spain all along. I told you about my grandmother when we first met. And of all of the people in the world, I thought you would understand. I cannot give up my war against Spain, just because the odds seem bleak."

"Jean, let other people fight Spain. There are many others now, the empire is crumbling, and you have served your part! The Floridas have been ceded to the United States and that is largely due to you. All these South American countries are declaring their independence. The Spanish Empire has known better days. Let it fall apart on its own. You are not a young man anymore. Why must you risk your life over and over again?"

She realized at once that this had been the wrong thing to say. She saw the wound to his pride in his dazed eyes.

"So that is it! You left your first husband, because he could not defend you. You chose me, not because you loved me, but because you needed a protector! Oh, I know, you went on and on about the passion you felt for me, but it would have meant nothing if I did not offer you security. And now you feel I am weak, and I cannot defend you, anymore."

"No, Jean."

"You are right. I can't defend you, anymore, and I cannot expect you to stay here and wait for me. It was wrong of me to leave you alone unattended. I can see that now. I have booked you a berth with the children, back to New Orleans. I am sending a draft to be drawn on my bank, and I will be instructing Ed Livingston on how to provide for your living expenses for the foreseeable future. You will want for nothing. Don't worry."

"No, Jean. That's not what I want."

"What *do* you want?"

"I want to go where you go. To live with you on your ship, if you must sail. I want us never to be apart."

He looked as if he were going to cry. "That's impossible. The ship does not belong to me. It belongs to the

State. And women are not allowed. And besides..." his voice cracked. "It would be too dangerous."

"Jean, are you hoping for death?"

"No. But we must plan for it, you and I, must we not? In the event of my death, one moiety of my fortune will be divided equally among Christina's children, Antoine, Lucien and Denise. The other half will go to you and Jules and Glenn. Please be assured that you will be well provided for."

"Why are you doing this?"

"These are your walking papers, Theodosia. Your severance pay. Your divorce. Your gat."

"My what?"

"It means that you are no longer bound by our oath, and you are free to seek another protector. I release you to all other men."

"But why?"

"Because if you will not come to my hanging, then you longer wish to be my wife."

He dropped the bundle of papers on the table, and he turned toward the door. "I sail tomorrow. Goodbye."

It was very quiet for a very long time. One could hear the neighbor's rooster crowing its twilight call, and the chickens cackling outside. She saw Jules staring at her, but preferred to ignore the question in his eyes.

On the one hand, she felt Jean had gone insane, punishing her just because she did not want to see him hanged. On the other, what he said made perfect sense. She really could not be expected to wait for him here in Cartagena. It would be no place to raise her children, especially if she were required to do it alone. She was a foreigner here, ill at ease and out of place, and she always would be. It would be better for her in New Orleans. She had always longed for a respectable little house in town like Marie Villard's, and only her pride had prevented her from admitting that the arrangement of plaçage for a quadroon was infinitely more secure than that of a white mistress with no contractual obligation to fall back on, in the event of abandonment.

But she didn't want a divorce, and she had seen the hurt in his eyes, and all that she wanted to do was to reassure him that he had not fallen in her regard.

"Maman, I think you should go and tell Papa that you will come to his hanging."

She laughed, a bitter, brittle laugh. "You think so, Jules?"

"Yes, Maman. It would mean a lot to him."

"Yes. Yes, it would."

"Hurry, Maman. He leaves tomorrow, and we may never see him again."

The wisdom in her little boy's words smote her heart. "Keep an eye on your brother," she said. And she took off in the night for the docks.

There were lanterns out on the deck of the *General Santander* when she finally found it.

"Madame Laffite! So good to see you."

It was Francisco Similien. It took her a moment to recognize him. "Francisco, what are you doing here?"

"Jean chose me as his quartermaster."

"Where is he now?" she asked, and seeing her troubled eyes, Francisco directed her to the captain's cabin. He knocked on the door and said: *"Juan, tienes una visita."*

"¿Quién es?"

"Es una surprisa." Francisco winked at her.

Jean opened the door and seemed confused to encounter her there, almost as if he did not know who she was.

"Jean forgive me," she said breathlessly and threw herself into his arms. "Of course, I will come to your hanging, if it means so much to you! I would come to your beheading or your impalement or your crucifixion with equal alacrity! Just don't send me away."

He laughed. "Are you sure? You really want to come to my hanging? I think you're lying."

She sighed. "I don't *want* you to hang, but if that's what *you* want, then I will be there with bells on."

"Is that what you think? That I want to be hanged?"

"I can't think of any other reason why you would be doing this now. Unless you have a death wish."

"I can't stop my war with Spain just because it is inconvenient. I can't forget about my grandmother."

"Is that what your grandmother asked of you? That you become a martyr?"

"No, of course not. That's not what she wanted at all."

"What *did* she want?"

"She wanted me and Pierre both to become scholars. She wanted us to take up the pen and not the sword."

"Then why didn't you?"

"Because I remembered the story of how her brothers, who were sailors, came and carried her away and saved her. And my grandfather, who was a scholar, could do nothing to help either her or himself. I decided to follow in the footsteps of my brother Alexandre and my uncle Reyné who were privateers. It was clear to me that the sword is mightier than the pen. And I wanted to avenge my grandmother."

"I don't think your grandmother would want to be

avenged like this. Are you sure she hated Spain? Wasn't that her home? The Inquisition and not Spain killed your grandfather. And the Inquisition has been dismantled. And... what's more, I have my doubts about your new employer. I don't see how Símon Bolívar is any better a master than King Ferdinand of Spain."

"Why do you say that, my love? What do you know about Bolívar?"

"Nothing except what you yourself have told me; that he confiscates private ships. That he wants a government monopoly on the waging of war. That he has outlawed privateering. How is he any better than Daniel Patterson? Or James Madison? Or even James Monroe?"

"He is no better, my love. Like them, he is a politician. Except for one thing; he accepts me into his country with open arms, and he grants me almost instantaneous naturalization and a commission in his fleet. Do you think, for one moment, that if I had been offered that by President Madison after the Battle of New Orleans, I would not be an American today?"

"You are American, Jean! You're more American than any of them!"

He laughed. "How can you say that?"

"Because you respect the constitution while they trample on it. Because you protected de Sedella's first amendment rights, when Andrew Jackson was going to order him to tell his parishioners how to pray. Because you spared the people of New Orleans the taxation that Alexander Hamilton put into effect, by smuggling in goods that we needed under the noses of the Revenue Service. Because you bypassed Jefferson's unlawful Embargo Act and allowed American businessmen to engage in trade. Because unlike the Second Bank of the United States, you have always paid your debts in specie. Because when you convene a tribunal and empanel a jury, due process is upheld as well as a speedy trial. Because you hang pirates, and they hang patriots. Because when America needed you the most you gave unstintingly, and you did not hold a grudge, and you fought right alongside your oppressors, and you saved us from certain annihilation!"

"But I can't do that now. They drove me away, and I'm no longer a captain of captains, and I can barely survive a simple sea battle, anymore. And *you* are looking for a new champion."

"No," she whispered. "I'm not. You will always be my hero! The only reason I said I would not come to your hanging was that I hoped to sway you. I thought that if I did not come to your hanging, there wouldn't *be* a hanging. I was just trying to save your life, Jean. Please, consider. It's time to quit."

"I can't stop now," he said stubbornly. "What kind of life would there be for me, if I stopped? I have been a privateer all my life. There is nothing else I can do."

"Really? And I thought you were an alchemist."

"Mock, if you will. I was just trying to impress you when we met. You were an educated lady, and I... don't have as much book learning as you. But you must know by now that I am not really an alchemist. My grandfather was an alchemist. But his secrets died with him. All I know how to do is mix gunpowder."

"Well, that is still something," she said. "Dupont de Nemours has made quite a fortune doing just that."

"I cannot give up privateering."

Softly she said it: "You already have." His heart was like a deer in her sights, and she didn't want to startle him, but she knew she must smite him with the truth.

"No. No, I haven't."

"Think, Jean. You have no ship of your own. You are working for somebody else – for the State. For Gran Colombia. And you once told me that you had no master and were accountable only to yourself. But … you are no better now than a ferryboat pilot who is paid a salary. You have lost your freedom! They've enslaved you."

There was a very long silence. She thought she could see the wheels turning in his head. Finally he got up, waved his arms about and declared: "You are right!"

She smiled. "Of course, I'm right."

Then he took a step back. "But … how can I continue with my war against Spain, unless I do so under cover of being a Colombian naval officer? I'll be hanged first before I give that up."

She sighed. "Jean, I don't want you to hang, because that is a fitting death for traitors and scoundrels and thieves. But you are none of these things. You should think of your children, before you decide you must die for the cause."

"My children will be well provided for. All of them. You have nothing to worry about on that account."

"That's not what I mean. I don't want them to see you hanged. It would be shameful."

"You have trouble accepting my humble origins. You do not want to see me hanged, because that is not a gentleman's death. You would rather see me drown at sea or die in battle or be shot in the head by a marksman than to see me hang. It is because you are ashamed that you chose a commoner and not a gentleman as your lover."

"No, Jean. That's not it at all. It's just that if the government of the United States of America hangs you, then this will be a great wrong, a great injustice crying out to be avenged. And who will avenge it? Jules and Glenn. And then they, too, will be lost without a country, without anyplace to call home. And I did so want for them to grow up to be American. Remember when you asked me once, if they had found my father guilty of treason and hanged him for a traitor, would I still be an American? I said I don't know. But I know now. I couldn't bear to see my country again, if they had done that. And I didn't want this to happen to Jules and Glenn. That's why I don't want you hanged and would rather see you die any other way."

Again, he was silent for some time. Finally he said: "I will take all this under consideration. But at dawn, I must sail as ordered."

Tears stood in her eyes. All her arguments had failed. Reason was on her side, and she knew that he knew it. And yet he was so stubborn.

"The only question that remains is whether you still wish to be my wife."

"Yes, Jean. I still do. And I will come to your hanging, though it breaks my heart."

He kissed her on the forehead and sent her away. "Francisco will escort you home," he said. "I still have work to do."

On February 23, 1823, Theodosia was summoned by Francisco Similien to come on board the *General Satander*, which was in the harbor again, because, he said, Jean had been mortally wounded. Hurrying on board, she found Jean in his cabin in bed, his head resting on the pillow.

"Jean, are you all right?"

"Don't come any closer. It's contagious."

"Your wound is contagious?"

"There is no wound, but I have a rather nasty cold." His nose sounded a little stopped up.

"A cold? Is that all?"

"No, that's not all. I also have an annoying rash all over my body."

"I thought you were dying!"

"That's what I wanted you to think."

"Why would you..!?"

"Sssh! No time to get angry. There is paper and ink and a pen on my desk. You will kindly take down what I have to say."

She sat down at the table and dipped the pen, but then looked up at him again. "Why do you need me to write for you?"

"I am already dead," he replied cryptically, "and it will not do for it to be written in my own hand. And besides, you will do so much better a job, since your spelling is superior to mine, even in a language you do not speak," he explained with a smile. "I trust you with this very important notice that I plan to send in to the *Gaceta Cartagena*."

"You are already dead?"

"No more questions, just write. *Combate Naval.*"

"Naval combat?"

"Don't translate, just write." He then proceeded with a stirring account of how a forty-three ton Colombian vessel, the *General Santandar*, under Captain Juan Laffite, gave chase to a Spanish schooner and a brig on th 2nd of February twenty leagues from the fort of Omoa in front of the Triumph of the Cross. And then all hell broke loose, shots were exchanged and...

"What in the world?"

"Keep writing. *A este tiempo el capitan Laffite,*

mortalmente herido, estimulaba el ardo de su tripulacion y encargo el mado de su corsario que sufrio la misma suerte."

"What are we writing here, Jean, a tragedy? First you get mortally wounded and now your second in command, too? Who is your second in command, by the way?"

"I'm leaving that open, in case Pierre would like to join me in faking his death."

"Ah."

"*El contramaestre, Francisco Similien, despues de la muerte del segundo continuo sosteniendo el combate hasta la uno de la noche.*"

"Well, that was nice of Francisco to keep up the good fight until one in the morning after your nameless mate died."

"Yes. Very. But by then the Spaniards were too tired, having felt themselves sorely mistreated by our guns. Put in something about that will you? And then we will finish it like this: *El capitan Laffite murio de sus heridos el siguiente dia. La perdida de este bravo oficial de marina es sensible, y el arrojo con lo que afrontó los fuerzas superiores que lo batieron manifiesta bien que entusiasta del honor quiso seguirlo en la senda de la muerte...*"

"The loss of this brave naval officer is moving. The boldness with which he confronted the superior forces manifests well that, as an enthusiast of honor, he wished to follow it down the road to death!" She laughed. "Oh, my love, you are *so* modest!"

"That's what I want it to say," he stubbornly insisted, like an author who would brook no editing. "Francisco will submit it to the paper."

She kissed him on the forehead with the obituary still in her hand.

"Be careful, or you'll catch my cold. Now give that to

Francisco and come back with the children. I have booked us a stateroom on a very nice passenger ship. We are traveling under the name of Lafflin. Oh, and Theo, rub some onion slices into your eyes, you don't want to be seen looking so happy."

⚜

"Where are we going, Papa?" It was Glenn who asked the question. They were standing on the deck, mere passengers on someone else's ship for the first time in years.

"Our destination is Charleston, South Carolina," Jean said. "That is in the United States."

"What will we do there, Papa?" Jules asked.

"I am planning to start a new gun powder making business, and I want to consult with some friends there how best to go about it. After that, we will travel to Saint Louis, which is in the newly formed State of Missouri. We will settle down close to where Denise and Frank are living."

"That will be wonderful!" Theodosia was so happy at the moment that everything Jean said seemed wonderful.

"Remember," he said to the boys. "we are traveling incognito."

"What does incognito mean?" Glenn asked

"It means no one must know who we are," Jules answered for Jean.

"But why?"

"It's a game we are playing," Jean said. "If anyone asks, our surname is Lafflin."

"Lafflin. That sounds funny! Like laughing!"

"Once you get used to it, it will not sound funny anymore." Jean turned from the boys to Theodosia. "And I think we should take some time to see our families. My father is aging now, and I plan to visit him one more time before it's too late. You should go see your father, too, in New York. Family is very important."

"Oh, I couldn't, Jean, I would be recognized."

"Then we will have him to visit us, once we are settled. Out in the new western states, no one will know him."

"Yes, yes that would be splendid." She turned to her children and said: "Would you like to meet your Grandfather Edwards?"

"If he is your father, Maman, and your maiden name is Mortimore, like you told me before, then why is his name Edwards?" Glenn asked. He was six years old now and starting to formulate difficult questions like his brother.

Theodosia was momentarily at a loss for an answer.

"Edwards isn't really his name," Jules answered for her. "It's just his traveling name, same as Lafflin is our traveling name."

"Oh."

"But his real name is Aaron Burr."

Theodosia was shocked. For a moment she was completely speechless. Then she turned to Jean accusingly: "Did you tell him that?"

Jean shrugged "No. I never did."

"Who told you that, Jules?"

"Why, you did, Maman." He smiled at her impishly.

"I don't remember telling you that."

"You told me to read between the lines. So I did."

She blushed. "Jules, do you know why I didn't want you to know about your grandfather?"

"Yes, Maman."

"Why?"

"Because you did not want me to know who *you* are.

But I already knew you were called Theodosia, because Papa never calls you Emma."

"But why? Why didn't I want you to know who I was? Do you know?"

"It is because when I was born you were still married to the Governor of South Carolina, but you loved Papa so much that you could not wait."

"How do you know this?" Her face was flushed. She was so ashamed.

"It was in the history book, about how you were captured by pirates. It was the very best part!"

"Jules, can you ever forgive me?"

Jules smiled. "But Maman, there is nothing to forgive." He gave her a big hug and added: "I am very much looking forward to meeting Aaron Burr. I have much to ask him." Then he turned to Glenn. "Come on, let's go talk to the captain now. Maybe he will show us his charts."

Glenn and Jules ran off, followed by Bandito, and Theodosia looked at Jean, who was smiling at her. "You see, you worry too much," he said.

"But Jean, now that he knows he's illegitimate, do you think it will affect him?"

"Why would it affect him?"

"Everyone knows that bastards have no sense of morality."

"Really?"

"Yes. It's true. Alexander Hamilton was a bastard, and he was just like the bastard son in all the plays I've ever read. And all the novels. Scheming. Manipulative. Underhanded."

Jean smiled. "I think you take the plays and novels you read entirely too seriously."

"But do you think it will affect Jules the way it did Alexander Hamilton? Do you think he'll..."

"Be cruel to women?" he completed for her.

"No, no. I don't think he would be," Theodosia answered her own question.

"Then what? Leave behind many fatherless children? Write salacious articles about public figures? Engage in slander or libel?"

Theodosia shook her head. "No, but it could be much worse than that. Oh Jean, do you think that it might lead Jules to favor centralized banking? Inflationary currency? Public debt?" she asked with trepidation.

Jean laughed. "I doubt it."

Epilogue
The Contribution

1844

Mrs. Smythe was on a tight schedule and was constantly checking the time. "Mrs. Lafflin, when did you say your husband was expected?"

"He should be here shortly. May I offer you another cup of tea?"

"No, I cannot stay much longer. I have been on a tour of all the states to drum up support for our cause, and it is only because you promised us a sizeable contribution that I took the trouble to visit with you today."

Theodosia looked down, hiding a smile. "Well, that is very blunt of you, Mrs. Smythe."

"When one is a woman on a mission, Mrs. Lafflin, one cannot afford to follow all the niceties. My only concern is with freeing the slaves. I do not care whose feelings are hurt in the process."

"Yes. Yes, of course. I fully support the cause, and my husband will be only too glad to write you a check."

"What did you say your husband does for a living, Mrs. Lafflin?"

"He manufactures gunpowder."

"Really? How distasteful!"

"Here, let me show you. It is a circular for my husband's business."

LAFFLIN, LAFFLIN & LAFFLIN

CARONDELET, MO

MANUFACTURERS

OF

GUNPOWDER

WHOLESALE & RETAIL

DEALERS IN FLINT

SAFETY FUSE FOR BLASTING

ORDERS PROMPTLY AND

FAITHFULLY ATTENDED TO

"Well, that is very impressive, Mrs. Lafflin, but..."

There was a sound toward the back of the house.

"Excuse me, Mrs. Smythe, but I think that I hear my husband. He is coming in through the mudroom. I will only be a moment."

She hurried to the back and scolded him in a whisper: "What took you so long? We don't want to make a bad impression on Mrs. Smythe."

"Well, if she wants my money, shouldn't *she* be making an effort to make a good impression on *me?*"

"You know how these Philadelphia intellectuals are, Jean."

"Yes, I do. I was only detained a little because a revenuer stopped by at the shop, and we got into a bit of a ... disagreement."

"A disagreement?"

"He accused me of running a distillery without paying the taxes on it, just because he saw my alchemical experiment for turning dirt into metal."

"Well, then you must have told him he was mistaken. Were you polite, Jean?"

"Yes, of course, I was. I am always polite. I started to tell him my theory about how we can turn dirt into base metals, and..."

"And what?"

"And he called me a liar. So I challenged him to a duel."

"You didn't?"

"I did."

"Oh, dear." She took a deep breath. "All right," she said, trying to be practical. "What did you do with the body?"

"Body? There was no body. He ran away."

She breathed a sigh of relief. "Oh, good! In that case, come and meet Mrs. Smythe."

He followed her into the parlor. "Mrs. Smythe, I would like to introduce my husband, John Lafflin."

"Enchanted," Jean said, leaning down and kissing her hand.

"Oh, well. How odd," Mrs. Smythe said, blushing a

244

little. "I understand you wish to make a contribution to our cause."

"Yes, I will be delighted to contribute to your most excellent cause," he said, and went to the sidetable where he took some time to write her a check, signing at the bottom *Jn Lafflin* in his familiar and inimitable hand.

"Oh, oh, Mr. Lafflin, this is so generous!" she exclaimed, once he had given it to her.

"Now, Mrs Smythe, a bit of advice. When you use this money to buy the freedom of any number of slaves, please make sure that you select for manumission people who are ready for liberty and will be able to earn their own living. For it would be very cruel indeed to set someone free who is not yet prepared."

"Oh, we're not using this money to set people free, Mr. Lafflin."

"No?" He looked puzzled. "But I thought that was your cause, Mrs. Smythe: freeing the slaves."

"Our cause is to put an end to the institution of slavery, which we believe is barbaric."

"Yes. Yes, it is barbaric," he nodded. "But what can we do, except set as many slaves free as we can afford to?"

"We are using our resources to lobby the politicians in Washington to emancipate all the slaves and to make slavery illegal."

"But I don't think the politicians in Washington have enough money to buy all the slaves and set them free. Think of the national debt!"

"Oh, they're not going to buy them, Mr. Lafflin."

"Well, what are they going to do, steal them?"

"They're going to pass a law that all the slaves are free."

"Just like that?"

"Yes, just like that."

"But that would constitute a taking of property without due process. Isn't that unconstitutional?"

"The constitution is not the final arbiter of what is moral, Mr. Lafflin."

"Are you some kind of radical, Mrs. Smythe? That does not sound like an American thing to say. I revere the constitution. I would do anything to uphold it. And I believe the policy you are pursuing would lead to civil war."

"Well, then Mr. Lafflin," she said huffily, the check in her hand, "if that is how you feel, why have you made this contribution to our Anti-Slavery League?"

He smiled. "Out of deference to my wife."

Once she had gone, Theodosia said: "Thank you, Jean. That meant a lot to me."

He sighed. "Do you remember when Jules paid Elmer twenty-five dollars to steal Mrs. Jones's slave?"

"Yes. He has always been such a good boy."

"Not a boy anymore. A man. And Denise has white hair now, whiter than yours. And five children."

She sighed. She thought about Glenn, who had died at twelve, and a shadow crossed her mind. They never mentioned him, because it made Jean so sad. So rather than upset him, she went back to talking about Denise, who would always and forever be the apple of her father's eye. "Yes, it's funny how things happen so fast. It seems like only yesterday that Frank was courting her. Everything is so different now. And the business has kept you so busy, we hardly ever go out, anymore. But I'm glad that we are making a difference with our good fortune."

"Theodosia, I am not sure any good will come of this anti-slavery league of yours. You may just have gotten me to contribute to the downfall of the Union."

246

"Oh, Jean. And what about all that money that you gave to Mr. Marx and Mr. Engels. You can't expect any good to come of that!"

"They were just very nice, idealistic men."

"A couple of Jacobins, if you ask me."

"Nonsense. They simply object to wage slavery. As do I. They think that everyone should have their own business, rather than working for somebody else."

"That's not what I got from what they said." She laughed. "I think they want the State to own all the businesses."

"No. You misunderstood them, Theo. They said that the workers should own the means of production. Just the way I own my gunpowder manufacting business, rather than working for Dupont de Nemours. And Frank owns his furniture business, rather than being employed in a big factory. And once upon a time, I owned a fleet of ships, which I used to defend this country and to fight Spain, rather than serving aboard a Navy vessel as a hireling."

"Jean, have you read Marx's manifesto?"

"No, my love. How could I read it? He hasn't finished writing it. And what there is of it to read is in German! How a man can live in Paris and insist on writing everything in German is beyond me!"

She laughed. "Well, let's hope he uses the money you gave him to have his writing translated, so people can judge for themselves what it is he is talking about. But I got the distinct impression he and Engels were no better than Simon Bolívar, confiscating ships and outlawing privateering and all manner of private enterprise."

They went out for a ride in their buggy through the streets of St. Louis, and on the side of the road, they saw several men who were passed out drunk.

"In my commune at Galveztown, I kept good discipline," Jean said. "There were no drunkards lying in the street, like here in St. Louis."

They drove on for a bit more, until Jean spotted a black man by a tobacconist's shop. "I know this man," he said. "I sold him at an auction years ago." And he left the reins to her and went to speak to his old acquaintance.

Theodosia was afraid for a moment. Jean was so trusting, and now that he was older, his hair streaked with silver, he seemed to her to be vulnerable in his simplicity. Wouldn't the man he had sold as a slave resent Jean? Wouldn't this be a good time to take revenge? But she saw that the old man smiled up at Jean, his toothless gums showing, and the two engaged in an animated conversation that lasted some time, as when two old friends meet after years of separation. Then Jean reached into his pocket and gave his old friend a pouch full of coins, and they hugged, and Jean came back to the buggy.

"Did he remember you?"

"Of course. How could he forget? Just as I remembered him."

"But aren't you afraid he'll turn you in?"

"Why would he do that?"

"For a reward?"

"Ah, there is no reward. They all think I died years ago. And besides, we are good friends. I found him a very good master, back in the days when I held auction at the Temple, and when his master died, he set him free in his will. He has a wife and children and grandchildren, all of them free and happy. We are just two old men who knew each other long ago, met again and reminisced about the good old days. You know, to Auld Lang Syne."

She smiled. "Yes, Jean. To Auld Lang Syne."

Frequently Asked Questions

1. **Did Theodosia Burr and Jean Laffite ever meet?**
   Could they have met? Could they have met at the
   time and place and in the manner described in
   Theodosia and the Pirates: The Battle Against
   ***Britain*? Could Theodosia have followed Jean to**
   Galveston as described in this book?

We don't know if they met. What we do know is that
they were contemporaries and that they had mutual
friends and acquaintances, among them Edward
Livingston and Andrew Jackson.

Theodosia Burr Alston boarded *The Patriot* on
December 31, 1812 and was never seen again
according to most historical reports. *The Patriot* and
all on aboard disappeared.

Could they have met with Jean Laffite aboard *La
Diligente*? Perhaps. It's a bit of a stretch, but in March
of 1813 Jean Laffite registered himself as captain of
"Le brig Geolette La Diligente" for a voyage to New
York. There is some unaccounted for time in the
Laffite saga that might allow for such an encounter in
early 1813. However, it is unlikely to have happened
on New Year's Day the way I describe in *Theodosia
and the Pirates: The Battle Against Britain*. Was
Theodosia ever at Galveston? We don't really know,
but there were some sightings reported.

2. **Did the Karankawa Indians have good relations**

with Jean Laffite? Were they cannibals? What exactly does it mean to be a cannibal?

According to the Journal of Jean Laffite the Karawanka helped him to rebuild after the hurricane of September 1818, but they took with them most of the supplies that Laffite had left at the time. The Karankawa lived off hunting and fishing. They were not cannibals, but they did occasionally eat some of their enemies' flesh in ceremonies involving magic. Cannibalism means eating your own kind. The Karankawa were not cannibals. They never ate each other.

3. **Were there really a Denise Laffite, a Francis Little and a Francis Neely the way I describe in this book?**

According to the Journal of Jean Laffite, Denise Jeanette Laffite was the privateer's third and last child by Christina Levine, and Francis Little was one of his captains who later became a furniture manufacturer. The Journal describes Francis Little accompanying Jean Laffite to meet with John Quincy Adams in November of 1818. The Journal also says the Denise married Francis Little after his retirement from privateering. Francis Neely was mentioned in the Journal as a captain who worked for both Laffite and Gambi. The romance and marriage and discord between Denise and Neely is entirely my invention. However, Jean Laffite did hang Francis Neely for piracy, according to the Journal.

Some historians do not believe that Denise

existed at all. William C. Davis is one of these, and in his book *The Pirates Laffite* he dispels the notion that Jean Laffite had a daughter. However, if you read the footnotes to Davis's book carefully (p. 618, fn 70), you will find that he cites documentary evidence that Jean Laffite, while on Galveston Island, summoned a Dr. Felix Formento to treat his daughter who was suffering from typhoid or yellow fever. Davis says categorically that it was not a daughter but a mulatto mistress who was sick, but if the person Jean Laffite claimed as a daughter had not been white, then some mention would have been made of this in the doctor's account, so I tend to believe that if Jean Laffite said it was his daughter, she was his daughter. No face saving would have been achieved by pretending that a mulatto mistress was his daughter.

4. **Who were the women in the Laffite brothers' lives? Was Pierre really married to Marie Villard?**
Jean has been associated, fictionally and historically, with a great many women, among them Christina Levine, Catherine Villard, Madeleine Rigaud and Emma Mortimore. However, there is no historical certainty concerning any of these liaisons.

Pierre's relationship under plaçage with Marie Villard is well documented in William Davis's book *The Pirates Laffite*.

In *Theodosia and the Pirates: The Battle Against Britain* I adopted the Davis version of Marie Villard's relationship with Pierre, while I borrowed the name Emma Mortimore from *The Journal of Jean Laffite* to serve as an alias for Theodosia. The real Emma Mortimore, if she existed, was much younger than Theodosia. In the Journal, Jean did not marry her until after he had retired, and she was about thirty years his junior. In *Theodosia and the Pirates: The War Against Spain* I mention the rumors about Catherine Villard and Jean. In this novel, I resolve the question by suggesting that many sightings of Jean with his daughter Denise have been misinterpreted as romantic liaisons with a "quadroon".

5. When did Jean Laffite's trip to speak with John Quincy Adams take place?

According to the Journal of Jean Laffite it was in November of 1818 that Jean set off to Washington, accompanied by Francis Little, to meet with John Quincy Adams. I took the majority of what transpired between the two men directly from the journal, adding only those measures that Jean offered Adams as a remedy to the Panic of 1819. While the Panic was not yet in full grip of the country, the ripples from the payment of the debt on the Louisiana Purchase and the consequent shrinking of the money supply could already be felt, and in some Eastern states the legislatures were already passing debtor relief acts. See Murray Rothbard's book, *The Panic of 1819,* for an in-depth discussion of what led to the Panic and how the people, the papers, and lawmakers reacted to it.

6. Did Aaron Burr receive a letter from General Toledo asking him to take command of the hispanic liberation movement?

Yes, he did. The letter, which is reprinted in an English translation in Matthew L. Davis's *Memoirs of Aaron Burr,* is dated September 20, 1816. Shortly thereafter General Toledo became reconciled with King Fernando of Spain and stopped working for a Mexican revolution.

If you are interested in exploring these and similar historical questions, please consider joining the forums at:

http://www.historiaobscura.com/

If you enjoyed reading *Theodosia and the Pirates: The War Against Spain,* please write a review of the book on Goodreads.com or Amazon.com. It will help more people to discover this book. And you can be sure that your review will be read and appreciated by the author!

For more on *Theodosia and the Pirates,* subscribe to my blog by that name:

http://theodosiaandthepirates.blogspot.com/

Suggested Reading

Arthur, Stanley Clisby. 1952. *Jean Laffite, Gentleman Rover.* New Orleans: Harmanson.

Davis, Matthew L. 1836. *Memoirs of Aaron Burr.* Online : http://www.gutenberg.org/catalog/world/readfile?fk_files=1468525

Davis, William C. 2005. *The Pirates Laffite: The Treacherous World of the Corsairs of the Gulf.* Harcourt: New York.

Hunt, Charles Havens. 1864. *Life of Edward Livingston.* D. Appleton and Co.: New York.

Kennedy, Roger G, 1999. *Burr, Hamilton and Jefferson: A Study in Character.*Oxford University Press: Oxford.

Laffite, John Andrechyne (or Jean Laffite?). 2009(1950 Or 1850?). The Journal of Jean Laffite: Moonglow Books:

Latour, Arsène Lacarrière. 2008 (1816). *Historical Memoir of the War in West Florida and Louisiana.* Editor, Gene Allen Smith. The Historic New Orleans Collection and University of Florida Press: Gainesville.

Rothbard, Murray N. 1962. *The Panic of 1819.* Auburn: Ludwig Von Mises Institute.

Saxon, Lyle. 1989. *Laffite the Pirate.* Gretna: Pelican.

About the Author

Aya Katz is the author of the novels *The Few Who Count*, *Vacuum County*, and *Our Lady of Kaifeng*, and of three books for children: *In Case There's a Fox*, *When Sword Met Bow*, and *Ping & the Snirkelly People*. Aya is an editor with Inverted-A Press and a primatologist with Project Bow, and when not entranced by derivational morphology, she is constantly trying to think of ways to conquer the world — without government involvement.

To learn more about her writing, and to find out when her next book has been published, please check Aya's Amazon author profile:

amazon.com/author/ayakatz